Praise for

EVERY EXQUISITE THING

"**The perfect summer read**. . . . Quick's prose
is so on point." —*InStyle*

"*Every Exquisite Thing* **lives up to the hype**. . . . You're going
to wish you could follow Quick's **awesome** heroine Nanette for
another 500 pages or so when you get to the end." —*Bustle*

"We loved how this new book nails both the rewards and the
pain that come with conformity and rebellion. **Perfect for
fans of John Green, Rainbow Rowell and, of course,
Matthew Quick!**" —*Justine*

★ "The author's **beautifully written** first-person narrative
captures the thoughts and feelings of a sensitive eighteen-year-old
girl struggling against the shallowness she sees around her. . . .
All of the elements of this novel work together to make this an
outstanding coming-of-age story." —*VOYA*, starred review

★ "Like the many anticonformity books before it, this **will
find a dedicated audience among teen readers**."
—*SLJ*, starred review

EVERY EXQUISITE THING

EVERY EXQUISITE THING

MATTHEW QUICK

LITTLE, BROWN AND COMPANY

New York • Boston

Copyright © 2016 by Matthew Quick
Excerpt from *Sorta Like a Rock Star* copyright © 2010 by Matthew Quick

Cover art copyright © 2017 by Neil Swaab. Cover design by Neil Swaab. Cover copyright © 2017 by Hachette Book Group, Inc.

Little, Brown and Company
Hachette Book Group
1290 Avenue of the Americas, New York, NY 10104
Visit us at lb-teens.com

Originally published in hardcover and ebook by Little, Brown and Company in May 2016
First Trade Paperback Edition: April 2017

Little, Brown and Company is a division of Hachette Book Group, Inc. The Little, Brown name and logo are trademarks of Hachette Book Group, Inc.

The publisher is not responsible for websites (or their content) that are not owned by the publisher.

The Library of Congress has cataloged the hardcover edition as follows:
Quick, Matthew, 1973–
	Every exquisite thing / by Matthew Quick. — First edition.
		pages cm
	Summary: Nanette O'Hare, a star student and athlete, is given a mysterious out-of-print cult classic novel by her beloved teacher that sparks the rebel within her, but as she befriends the reclusive author and attempts to insert her true self into the world with wild abandon, Nanette learns the hard way that sometimes rebellion comes at a high price.
	ISBN 978-0-316-37959-5 (hardcover) — ISBN 978-0-316-37958-8 (ebook) — ISBN 978-0-316-37962-5 (library edition ebook) [1. Books and reading—Fiction. 2. Self-realization—Fiction. 3. Authors—Fiction. 4. Teacher-student relationships—Fiction.] I. Title.
	PZ7.Q3185Ev 2016
	[Fic]—dc23

2015011641

ISBNs: 978-0-316-37961-8 (pbk.), 978-0-316-37958-8 (ebook)

Printed in the United States of America

LSC-C

10 9 8 7 6 5 4 3 2 1

For the green bench near the creek

PART ONE

1

He Was an Adult and I Was Still a Kid

The last lunch period before Christmas break junior year, when I arrived at Mr. Graves's classroom, he was full of holiday cheer and smiling much more than usual. We had been eating alone together for months. But for that day, his wife had baked me a plate of Italian pizzelle cookies, which made me wonder what Mr. Graves had been telling her about me. The cookies looked like giant snowflakes and tasted like black licorice. We each had one, and then Mr. Graves handed me a small box wrapped in blue paper dotted with the white silhouettes of reindeer equipped with enormous antlers. I had never received a present from a teacher before. It seemed significant.

"Just a little something from one cafeteria avoider to another," he said, and smiled.

I tore into the wrapping paper.

Inside was a paperback novel called *The Bubblegum Reaper*, written by Nigel Booker. The cover was taped to the spine, and the pages had yellowed. It smelled like an old camping tent that had remained slightly damp for fifty years. On the white front was one of those long Grim Reaper scythes with the curved blade at the top, only it was made entirely of rainbow-colored gumballs—like someone had arranged them that way on white marble. The image was certainly weird. It both frightened and lured.

I opened the book to the first page.

The dedication read "For the archery pit."

Bizarre, I thought.

I quickly flipped through the dog-eared pages and saw that someone had underlined hundreds of passages throughout.

"I read that book when I was your age, and it changed my life," Mr. Graves said. "It's out of print. Probably worth some money, but it's just not the type of book you sell. I scanned the entire thing and made a digital file a long time ago. And I promised myself that I'd pass my copy on to the right student whenever he or she came along. It's maybe not the most literary work in the world. Probably a bit dated. But it's a cult classic and I have a feeling that it might be the perfect read for you. Maybe even a rite of passage for people *like us*. Anyway, Merry Christmas, Nanette O'Hare."

When I gave Mr. Graves a thank-you hug, he stiffened and

said, "No need for all that." Then he laughed nervously as he gently pushed me away.

His doing that made me angry at the time, but later I sort of got why he was being cautious. He saw what was coming before I did, because he was an adult and I was still a kid.

I began reading that night.

2

Like the Story Wasn't Finished

The Bubblegum Reaper is about a boy who identifies himself as Wrigley because he's addicted to Wrigley's Doublemint chewing gum. He says it calms his nerves, and he chews so furiously (and often) that he frequently gets jaw aches and even "the occasional bout of lockjaw." He never tells you his real name as you follow him through a year of high school.

Wrigley mostly observes his classmates, whose company he doesn't enjoy, and talks about "quitting" all the time, only you really don't know what he wants to "quit." I Googled the book and there are theories online—whole websites dedicated to answering the question. Some people think Wrigley wants to kill himself, thereby quitting the human race. Some believe he simply wants to drop out of school. Some people think Wrigley's talking about God and really wants to quit believing in a higher power, which I'm not sure I get, because the narrator doesn't mention God even once. There are others who theorize that Wrigley wants to quit America and that the whole book is about communism, but again, I'm not sure I believe that, either.

The problem is that Wrigley falls in love with one of two identical twin sisters named Lena and Stella Thatch, only he doesn't know which he loves. It happens because one of them likes to talk to this turtle that suns itself on a rock sticking out of the creek near the high school they attend. Wrigley names this turtle Unproductive Ted because it just sits on the rock all day long doing nothing but soaking up the sun. (I love that nickname so much: Unproductive Ted.) From behind an oak tree, Wrigley eavesdrops on the twin talking to Unproductive Ted about all her fears and worries and about something awful her father had done, but you never quite know for sure what that is. What's certain is that this girl is on the verge of tears the whole time. Wrigley listens patiently to everything the girl needs to get out, and then once he shows himself and she realizes he's heard everything, Wrigley immediately tries to comfort the twin by saying, "What you just said. All of it. I understand. I really do. I think the same thoughts—well, most of them—too." She's mad at first about "the spying," but then she and Wrigley have this amazing talk about life and their school and how they can't be honest "outside the woods" and about "just quitting."

The tragedy manifests when Wrigley leaves her. On his way

home, much to his horror, he realizes he didn't ask for a name and therefore doesn't know if he had this really intimate experience with Stella Thatch or Lena Thatch, which induces a crippling and nauseating anxiety attack—he actually pukes—because the twin kept saying over and over, "Please don't tell my sister about this. *Please!*" He realizes that he can't ask one of the twins if it was her by the creek without risking betraying her confidence, because if he asks the wrong twin, it would "ruin everything." It's obvious that he can't get out of his own way, but you feel really sorry for him anyway because in his mind it is an unsolvable problem that tortures him.

He spends months trying to figure out exactly which twin he spoke with and waiting for her to say something to him in school and worrying that maybe *she's waiting for him* to make the first move, and he's also worrying even more that she regrets their private conversation in the woods and never wishes to speak with Wrigley again.

Finally, after months of watching the two twins in the lunchroom, he decides that Lena is his twin, mostly because she sometimes taps her foot nervously when she speaks at the table full of popular girls, but he's not exactly sure. Furthermore, Lena has begun carrying a handbag with an *L* stitched into it, which also seems like a very good sign. Maybe she's sending him a signal about her identity, clueing him in, he thinks.

Wrigley decides to ask Lena to the prom, telling himself that if she says yes, he will know for sure that she was the one who confessed to Unproductive Ted. She does say yes but seems unenthusiastic about the proposal, which confuses him even more.

Wrigley rents a tuxedo and buys a yellow rose wrist corsage, and yet, just before he rings the doorbell at the twins' home, he realizes that the twin he met in the woods would never want to go to the prom—he knows this because he doesn't really want to go to the prom, either, and is only in a tuxedo to find out if he has the right sister. He couldn't care less about any of the rest, or what he calls "pageantry." The twin who talks to a turtle all alone by the creek would not love the Wrigley who attends the prom, because he is in a costume and is not being true to who he really is—the "plainly clothed Wrigley in the woods." It's so obvious, he thinks, and I agree. He cannot attend the prom. It would ruin any chance he had of a true relationship with the right twin.

Wrigley decides that he has failed before he has even begun, and so he doesn't ring the doorbell but goes to the spot where he and the twin first spoke, thinking that the real sister might be there waiting and maybe they'd talk and end up kissing like at the end of a modern fairy tale. Instead, he finds a bunch of elementary school kids using sticks to spin Unproductive Ted around on the back of his shell, "his four legs cutting a cruel circle in the air, as if he were a turtle top." Wrigley flies into a rage, grabs the biggest of the kids, and screams "WHY? WHY? WHY?" over and over again.

The elementary-school-kid ringleader says he was only having a little fun and they weren't going to actually kill the turtle, so Wrigley sticks his gum in the kid's hair, throws him into the creek, and says, "I'm only having a little fun, too, but I won't actually hold you underwater until you turn blue and drown."

Then he holds the kid's head underwater until his friends start to plead for their buddy's life, begging Wrigley to let him breathe again. When the half-drowned kid resurfaces soaking wet, he gasps and begs not to be held underwater again. Wrigley lets him go, and the kids run away.

Unproductive Ted bites Wrigley's hand and removes a triangle of skin when our hero sets the turtle upright.

As Unproductive Ted makes his escape, Wrigley bleeds and drip-dries and curses and waits for the right twin to show up, but she never does.

The parents of the kid he almost drowned arrive instead, and the father throws Wrigley into the creek and starts kicking water up into Wrigley's face, saying, "How do you like being a bully now? My son is eleven years old and half your size. You're a scumbag. A complete and utter embarrassment to the community. Why aren't you at the prom, anyway? You already have the tuxedo on! It's un-American to skip the prom. Are you a pinko communist?"

Rather than explain himself, Wrigley strips out of his prom costume, swims into the middle of the polluted creek, where he knows "no one will follow," floats naked on his back, and says, "Now I understand, Unproductive Ted, why you sit alone on the rock all day long doing nothing. I quit. I'm just going to float here forever and ever and ever." And then the novel ends with Wrigley laughing maniacally as the stars begin to pop through the night sky above.

On the Internet, there are different theories about the ending, but the predominant thought is that Wrigley is rejecting conventional society—family, government-run school, even his sexuality—to just be in that moment, floating unclothed in the creek.

Some say it's a lesson in Zen Buddhism and that Wrigley maybe even experiences enlightenment.

It felt like the story wasn't finished, which upset me because I wanted to know what happened to Wrigley after he got out of the water. I even reread the book three times over Christmas break thinking I had missed something.

3

You've Got to Meet Him Yourself

When school started up again in January, I was waiting in the hallway with my back against Mr. Graves's classroom door.

"Did you sleep here last night, Nanette? The sun isn't even up yet," he joked when he arrived.

"What happens to Wrigley?" I asked. "I have to know. Because Wrigley is me. And it just can't end like that. It. Just. Can't."

"Why not?"

"Because I need more."

"Always leave them wanting more. That's one of the great rules of show business."

"This isn't show business. This is *literature*. And it's my life, too," I said. "This book is *me*. Me. It's so much more than a story. The author has a responsibility to provide answers. *All* the answers!"

Mr. Graves smiled, laughed, and said, "I thought you would like *The Bubblegum Reaper*. Like I said—a rite of passage for weirdos like us."

Mr. Graves was always using the word *weirdo* to describe himself and people he liked. He said that all the great writers were "weirdos," too—that our best artists, musicians, and thinkers were first labeled *weird* in high school or "when they were young." That was "the price of admission."

"Why is it called *The Bubblegum Reaper*, anyway?" I said.

"Why do you think?"

"I have no idea. That's why I'm asking you!"

He laughed. "Well, there are many theories."

"I did an Internet search already. I'm not buying what's out there."

"Then maybe you should ask the author yourself."

"How can I do that?"

"Mr. Booker actually lives within walking distance of this school. Did you know that?"

"Are you even serious?"

Mr. Graves smiled like he had been leading me down a path without my knowing it. "And I hear that if you offer to buy him a cup of coffee at the House, he'll speak with you. Although I should warn you that he never, ever gives a straight answer. And I think he actually hates *The Bubblegum Reaper* now."

"How do you know that?"

"Because I wrote him many letters when I was a teenager, until he finally met with the sixteen-year-old me."

"What did he say?"

"Oh, I'm not going to spoil it for you. You've got to meet him yourself. It's definitely *an experience*. One that I'm pretty sure I can arrange for you. That is—if you're game."

4

A Hymn to the Noble Art of Quitting

I was most definitely game.

Mr. Graves made the arrangements, and I soon found myself sitting down across from Nigel Booker, the author of my new favorite book. The House is the local coffee place, and it's only about six blocks from my actual domicile. You'll find mostly older people in there, which doesn't bother me one bit, because I'm not all that fond of my generation, truth be told.

"Ms. O'Hare?" he said when he arrived. When I nodded, he extended his hand. I shook it, and he said, "Call me Booker. I'm not a *mister* type." He was older than Mr. Graves by a few decades. Tufts of white hair sprouted from his gigantic ears. Plaid pants that were too short at the bottom and too baggy around the waist. His oversize cable-knit wool sweater was worn and a bit dirty. And he had hair slicked back on the sides and poufed up at the top like Elvis—only gray. "You really want to buy this old man coffee?" he said, pointing his thumbs back at his face. "How did I get so lucky?"

I nodded, and then we ordered and I paid, and we sat down.

"So?" he said.

I took a deep breath and said, "*The Bubblegum Reaper* is my new personal manifesto. I didn't know that there were other people like me, but there obviously are. And you get it, too. Which is why—"

"Okay," he said, and then chuckled. "That's enough of that."

I couldn't tell if he was just being modest, so I pressed on with my questions. "Why isn't it in print anymore?"

"Probably because it isn't very good," he said, and then laughed. "I didn't have any formal training as a fiction writer. I just had this story in my head and I had to get it out. It was like I had a fever one summer and the writing was the medicine. I couldn't believe it got published, and I have no idea why I sent it to New York in the first place. Probably a double case of temporary insanity—me *and* the obscure publisher, which went out of business shortly after the book came out. Go figure. They only had time to do one moderate-sized paperback print run. Thank God."

I had no idea what he was talking about, so I stuck to the questions I had prepared ahead of time. "Is it true that you buy all the used copies off the Internet and burn them?"

He laughed and said, "I don't even have an Internet in my home."

The way he said "an Internet" made me believe he was telling the truth. You can always tell when an old person has no idea what you are talking about, because they mess up the wording almost as if they're trying to defeat the thing you are discussing by refusing to name it correctly. I call this technique senior-citizen word voodoo.

I went to my third question, saying, "What happens to Wrigley after he gets out of the creek?"

"Who says he ever gets out?"

"So he drowns?"

"We can't know for sure."

"Why?"

"The story ends."

"But you could write more."

"No, I can't. There's no more to write."

"Why?"

"Just the way it is. The story ends where it ends."

"I don't understand."

"See that nice woman who served us our coffee?"

I looked back over my shoulder at the tall cashier with the brown ponytail and the permanent smile on her face, and I nodded.

"Her name is Ruth," Booker said. "Ever see her before?"

Kids my age never came into this coffee shop, so I said, "No."

"Maybe you won't ever see her again."

"So?"

"You only got to see five minutes of Ruth's story. And that's just the way it is. But Ruth, well, she goes on now whether you're looking or not. She does all sorts of things that some people see and some don't. But your version of Ruth's story will be the five minutes you spent buying coffee from her. That's just the way it is."

"All right," I said. "But what does that have to do with *The Bubblegum Reaper*? Ruth is real. Wrigley's a fictional character."

"There are no such things as fictional characters."

"What?"

He sipped his coffee, smirked, and said, "I wrote that book a long time ago. Before you were even born. It's hard to remember what I was thinking back then. I can hardly remember what I was thinking this morning. You seem like an intelligent young person. You don't need me to explain anything to you."

My head was spinning, so I went back to my prepared list of questions. "What did you mean when you said Wrigley wanted to quit? In the book. He kept saying he wanted to quit. *Quit what?*"

He raised his eyebrows and said, "Don't you ever feel like you want to quit doing something everyone else makes you feel like you're *supposed* to keep doing? Didn't you ever just simply want to ... *stop?*"

"I don't know, I mean, I guess so," I told him, even though I knew exactly what he meant.

A silence hung between us—like when you suddenly notice the dust motes dancing all around you in the late-afternoon sun and you wonder how the hell you didn't notice them before.

"Why don't we talk less about my failed attempt to be a novelist and more about you?" he finally said. "Are you a happy person?"

I'm not sure anyone had ever bothered to ask me that before, so I said "What do you mean?" to buy time and think of a clever answer.

I mean—when was the last time someone asked if you were happy and then looked you in the eyes in a way that made you feel as though they actually gave a shit about your response?

"Do you enjoy all that you are participating in?" he said.

"Like—do I want to quit anything?"

"It's not a crime to admit such things. The Participation Gestapo isn't hiding behind that plant over there. No Participation KGB, either. This is America. You are free to utilize freedom of speech—*freedom, period*. And I already know you want to quit something or you wouldn't be so interested in my stupid little book, which is—at the end of the day, if I remember correctly—a hymn to the noble art of quitting. So let's have it. What do you want to quit more than anything else in the world?"

"Soccer," I said, surprising myself, although it was absolutely true. I'd hated soccer for a long time.

"Soccer. Okay. Now we're getting somewhere. Next question: Why?"

"I don't know."

"Oh, I bet you do. Are you on the school team?"

I looked down at the counter, noticed the white grains of sugar scattered around the table. "I'm the captain and leading scorer."

"So you're good at it?"

"Sort of," I said, even though I made the All–South Jersey Team as a sophomore, colleges were recruiting me, and scouts came to my games. But I didn't really care about any of that. The attention was embarrassing. Made me feel like even more of a fraud.

"I bet no one ever told you this truth before, so here it is for the price of a cup of coffee." He took a sip and then stared into my eyes before saying, "Just because you're good at something doesn't mean you have to do it."

We locked eyes for a second.

He smiled like he was giving me the secret to life.

Try telling that to my coach and my father, I thought. I shook my head and then said, "I wanted to kill those little kids who were spinning around Unproductive Ted. And then I wanted to kill the kid's dad, who throws Wrigley into the creek. And I'm not a violent person at all. I won't even let my mom set mousetraps. Never been carded in my entire soccer career. No reds. No yellows. I've never wanted to kill *anything* before. Not even a weed or a spider. But you made me feel such intense feelings. The ending of your book made me so incredibly angry."

Booker smirked in this awfully sad way and then looked out the window at nothing in particular. "Oh, please don't blame me for your hatred. It was there before you cracked open my *Bubblegum* book. I can assure you of that. It's in all of us. We at least need to take responsibility for our own share—especially whatever we let leak out."

"I'm not trying to..." I said, but then stopped because I realized I was.

"You should read Bukowski's 'The Genius of the Crowd,'" he said, reestablishing eye contact. "That poem has a thing or two to say about hatred."

"Who?"

"The great Charles Bukowski. Hero of nonconformists and blue-collar poets the world over."

My family certainly wasn't blue-collar, but I liked the sound of *nonconformist*.

I asked him how to spell the last name and typed the letters into my phone. Then I typed *The Genius of the Crowd* in, too, which I later read and loved. Reading that poem was like putting on the proper prescription glasses after bumping into walls for my entire life. Bukowski was able to sum up precisely what I had been feeling for many years, and he made it look so easy on the page.

"Be careful with the Buk's poems," Booker said that day in the coffee shop. "Powerful stuff. And please—whatever you do— don't tell your parents I told you to read counterculture poetry, especially if they're uptight types who send out family portraits as Christmas cards. Definitely don't say a word about the Buk if they make you coordinate holiday outfits. Even non-Christmas-card-sending suburban parents tend to despise Charles Bukowski, which, of course, is why so many suburban kids love him."

"How did you know they do that?" I asked, astonished. "My parents. The Christmas cards. Coordinating holiday outfits."

"Far too often, people are woefully predictable. And I know many things. It's a curse. Here's something else I know: You are not doomed to be your parents. You can break the cycle. You can be whoever you want to be. But you will pay a price. Your parents and everyone else will punish you if you choose to be you and not them. That's the price of your freedom. The cage is unlocked, but everyone is too scared to walk out because they whack you when you try, and they whack you hard. They want you to be scared, too. They want you to stay in the cage. But once you are a few steps beyond the trapdoor, they can't reach you anymore, so the whacking stops. That's another secret: They're too afraid to follow. They adore their own cages."

I opened my mouth to defend my parents because they really are good people, and I didn't want him to believe that they whacked me, even metaphorically, but for some reason, no words came out of my mouth. The afternoon had gotten intense much too quickly.

"You seem like a weird, lonely girl, Nanette O'Hare. I'm a weird, lonely old man. Weird, lonely people need each other. So let's just cut to the chase." He smiled and took another sip of his coffee. Then he said the seven words that would change my life forever. "Would you like to be my friend?"

I nodded a bit too eagerly and was shocked to feel myself welling up.

"Well, I never under any set of circumstances whatsoever discuss *The Bubblegum Reaper* with my friends. So once we make it official, that's it. We never talk about Wrigley or Unproductive Ted or the Thatch twins or any of it ever again. *Understood?*"

I had one more question prepared—and maybe to stop myself from crying, I asked, "Before I become your friend, then—on the Internet, I read that several publishing companies have offered to rerelease the book and you turned them all down. Is that true?"

"Yes."

"Why?"

"Because I own the copyright and can do whatever the hell I want with it. I chose to quit publishing. I made that decision a long time ago. Publishing *The Bubblegum Reaper* was the biggest mistake of my life."

"You want to quit—*like Wrigley?*"

"Yes! So can we end all this literary talk and simply be friends already? True friends are better than novels! Better than Shakespeare plays! Any hour of the day! Fake friends, on the other hand—well, I'd rather smash open my skull with a solid-gold Bible than endure the slow poison of a fake friend!" When a few other patrons looked over at us, Booker thumbed his nose at them and then smiled at me.

I laughed. "Is this just a way for you to get me to stop asking questions about your book?"

"No, it's a way to move beyond the book. The book's there—stagnant. It never changes. We evolve as people. I'm not the same man who wrote that book twenty-some years ago. And you won't be the same girl in love with Wrigley forever."

I blushed because he was right about one thing: I absolutely was in love with Wrigley. I'd even begun hanging around the pond in our town where turtles sun in the summer because I was secretly hoping that Wrigley would magically show up—like I could think him into existence, as we do when we read fiction. I felt my cheeks burn and changed the subject by saying, "So why did you agree to meet me today? If you hate talking about your book so much?"

"I love free coffee in real cups and saucers," he said without missing a beat. "Buy me a cup of black and I will meet you every single week forever and ever."

I smiled and pushed a strand of hair behind my ear. "What happens when we become friends?"

"No way to tell now. I think we just have to give it a try and find out. There are no guarantees when it comes to such treacherous things as friendship. It's a tricky business."

"You were Mr. Graves's friend when he was my age, right?"

"We corresponded. Yes."

Mr. Graves was one of the few adults I admired. I wanted to do whatever helped make him the person he turned out to be.

"Okay," I said. "We're friends now."

"Good."

And that was it.

Booker and I became friends.

We met regularly—sometimes for coffee at the House, sometimes in his garden, where he has a pet turtle named Don Quixote who sits eternally between two miniature windmills that have faces and arms holding swords, which makes Booker laugh and laugh every time he looks at his pet, which is daily. Initially, we didn't talk about his book even once, although I continued to reread it dozens of times. I kept my word, even though I also kept accidentally calling Don Quixote "Unproductive Ted," which made Booker angry. "That's not his name!" he'd yell whenever I slipped up.

And if you are one of those pessimistic people who think that an old man can't befriend a teenage girl without some sort of perverted, deviant ulterior motive, let me end the witch hunt right here and now. Booker was as grandfatherly as they come and never once did or said anything inappropriate or sleazy. No funny business at all ever went on between us. I loved him like I loved walking through summer grass barefoot, like I loved a warm mug in my palms, like I loved driving on a long road as the sun sets in the distance. It was a good, safe, simple sort of friendship—well, at first, anyway.

5

He Never Told Anyone Else What I Did

It was our usual lunch period, except it was Valentine's Day. Mr. Graves and I were alone in his classroom, talking about Booker. We had turned two desks sideways and were watching a flock of birds perching on the wires just outside the windows. We were also laughing and smiling and trading info like old friends. He turned to say something at the same time I did. Our faces were so close—I could smell his aftershave and see where his razor had irritated his neck just below his jawbone—and when I looked up into his eyes, suddenly I was full of electricity.

I didn't plan to do what I did next.

That was when whatever we had ended. And I'm pretty sure it was why he quit teaching at the end of the year, too.

It just sort of happened spontaneously, like when you see a spider crawling up your bedroom wall and you reflexively shiver. Or maybe like the first time you accidentally stumble upon Internet porn and your skin tingles and you want to stop looking, but you just can't, and so you click on more and more links.

I clicked Mr. Graves's link without his permission.

I shouldn't have done it. I don't know what happened, but it cost me. I'll never forgive myself. The worst part was that I knew I was ruining everything as I leaned in, and yet I didn't stop. He turned his head away at the last possible second and I kissed his cheek. His face reddened as he removed my hand from his neck, and then he whispered, *What are you doing?* When I tried to let him know I could keep the secret with a smile, he yelled at me, saying, "You can't do that! *Ever!* Do you understand, Nanette? You've crossed a line." His words felt like a slap across the mouth. I suddenly felt so stupid. When I started crying, I couldn't stop. I sobbed and sobbed. He used the phone in his classroom to call for the nurse. I didn't even know her name, but she came and led me to her office, and I got to lie in a bed surrounded by a white curtain and feel guilty for the rest of the day. I told her I had cramps, and she didn't ask any further questions.

The next day, Mr. Graves's door was locked during his lunch period and the lights were off. I peeked through the little rectangular window, and no one was in there. My attempted kiss had driven him to the dreaded teachers' lounge, a place he had often told me he hated, saying, "Some teachers are even worse than the students when it comes to making their peers feel awful." He never told anyone else what I did—or at least I was never called down to the principal's office—and I never heard about it again.

He wouldn't even look at me in class, and then one day I was suddenly transferred out. My adviser, Mr. Bryant, wouldn't tell me why, but his stiff, awkward manner made me feel like I was Abigail Williams in *The Crucible*.

After some time had passed, I stopped by Mr. Graves's room between periods and, standing in the doorway, asked him if we could speak. In a cold, distant voice, he said we could meet at the school counseling office if Mr. Bryant was present, and that was when I knew I'd never share another private lunch with my favorite teacher ever again, that whatever we'd had was dead and gone forever.

And I was right.

6

Living in a Regularly Updated Catalog

My parents never were bad people, at least according to modern American standards. They fed me. They took me shopping in the most expensive clothing stores so that I looked like everyone else at my school whose parents had money. They made sure we lived in one of the best school districts in the state and maybe even the country. They never abused me in any way and were always encouraging me to do what they thought I wanted to do, but that was the big problem. I didn't want to do what I was initially doing as their daughter. Only I never told anyone.

My mother is an interior designer. She's still attractive and is constantly updating her wardrobe, which means we shopped for new clothes at least twice a week. All through high school, we also used to go on these mother-daughter dates every Sunday morning, where we'd have brunch in the city and then go to the opera or maybe a movie or more shopping. I liked going. I really did. But then my mother began to use this time to make confessions to me, like we were sisters or friends rather than mother and daughter. I remember one time when we were seated at a window table on the top floor of the Bellevue, sipping mimosas—Mom tipped the waiters very well, so they never even blinked whenever she ordered two mimosas, regardless of the fact that I was obviously underage—and my mother said, "Does the way your father eat ever bother you?"

"What do you mean?" I asked.

"The way he munches and breathes through his mouth at the same time so everyone can see what's inside. Like he's a cow chewing its cud. He does that even in restaurants. I've tried to bring it up only to save him from his own embarrassment, but he flies into a rage now whenever I even mention the word *chewing*."

I scanned my memory and couldn't think of a single moment when my father's chewing had annoyed me, nor could I remember my mother ever speaking about it directly to him, even though we ate dinner together as a family every night. And this was when I realized that my parents had a secret life independent of me—that they fought when I wasn't looking or behind the bedroom door in whispers maybe and then put on a show when I was around. I understood this chewing conversation about my father was going to be a turning point for me. Maybe you think I'm stupid because it took me so long to figure out that my parents really didn't love each other anymore, but I had always believed that my parents were exactly who they appeared to be. Why would I think any different?

I started to notice other things about Mom—like how she could be in the most miserable mood, complaining about every aspect of her life as we were shopping for groceries, and then she would run into one of her clients in the cereal aisle and her entire demeanor would immediately shift. "Hello, Mrs. So-and-So!" she'd practically sing as if she were suddenly in a musical. A smile would bloom on her face, and her eyes would open so wide they looked like they might fall out of the sockets. Mom always asked about the woman's family loudly and then brought up some sort of personal tragedy in a co-conspirator's whisper—such as bad medical news or a husband's drinking problem or a neighbor the woman hated—before Mom would work in a decorating project that "really should be taken care of immediately if you want to maintain the resale value of your home because, after all, *updating is the best investment in your most important investment.*" Mom was always going on about how a family's home is the most valuable thing they owned, and yet so many people didn't invest with fashionable updates. "Ridiculous!" she'd yell when it was just her and me. "Asinine!"

I remember vividly a time when all this happened in the food court at the mall. We ran into Mrs. Shaeffer and her daughter Rebecca, who was in my class, but no one really knew Rebecca, because she was always out of school with severe asthma. If she showed up at school seven times a year, that was a lot. Mom asked Rebecca a million questions about her health, to the point where I was starting to get embarrassed because it was painfully clear that Rebecca didn't want to talk about it. I remember she kept taking hits of her inhaler after every answer she gave, even though she didn't seem to be out of breath. The funny thing was that Mrs. Shaeffer watched the conversation with this look that suggested she absolutely loved my mom, simply because Mom was asking her sick daughter questions and looking concerned. Maybe no one else spoke to Rebecca ever. I don't know. But once Mom finished with Rebecca, she made her move, saying to Mrs. Shaeffer, "So—are you ready to bring that Windex-blue kitchen out of the nineteen seventies and into the twenty-first century? You'll double your investment when you sell your house. Guaranteed. Money in the bank."

It seemed like Mrs. Shaeffer didn't care all that much about updating her kitchen or selling her home, but she didn't want to disappoint my mother, either. I remember thinking that Mom was bullying her into spending a lot of money on something that Mrs. Shaeffer seemed sort of indifferent about. And it was the first time I ever really disliked my mom. I hated her a little bit that day, even though I fully realized that it was her job to sell, and her ability to persuade people to update their homes was what paid for the lifestyle we enjoyed—only I wasn't really enjoying "our lifestyle" deep down inside, and I was beginning to believe that neither were Mom and Dad.

When we walked away from them, Mom looked back over her shoulder to make sure Mrs. Shaeffer and Rebecca were out of earshot, and then she said, "If you're too sick to attend school, how can you be in the mall gorging on Chinese stir-fry? It's disgusting the way she lets her daughter put on so much weight and blames asthma. So much of life is mental, Nanette. Remember that. I'm glad I don't have to worry about your mind—*or your physique.* How did we get so lucky?"

"Why did you push Mrs. Shaeffer so hard to remodel her kitchen?" I asked, and just as soon as the words were out of my mouth, I regretted saying them, fearing that my mother would take it as an attack.

Without missing a beat, Mom said, "I bring beauty, class, and style into the homes of otherwise unremarkable women. Help their self-esteem. Did you know scientific research has proved that a married couple's sex life improves after a home is redecorated? It's true."

It was obvious that my mother completely believed this and was now selling to me, so I didn't say anything else, even though I secretly wanted to live in an old, outdated home that felt lived in and full of mystery and history and magic—unlike our home, which was sort of like living in a regularly updated catalog. I didn't want to imagine what that did or didn't do for my parents' bedroom experience.

My dad does something with the stock market for a living, but I'm not exactly sure what. He's always talking about the ups and downs of the various economies around the world the way other people talk about the weather, and I get the sense that the "global economy" is just some never-ending story adults tell themselves. I understand the basic stock market principle of "buy low and sell high," but that's about it, even though my father has tried to get me more interested in my portfolio.

I started playing soccer when I was five years old. All the girls in my neighborhood were on a team called the Rainbow Dragons. I liked the smell of grass and being outside and eating orange wedges at halftime. It was nice that everyone came to watch, and it was fun to kick the ball as hard as you could. For some reason, I could kick the ball more accurately than everyone else, and I started to score just about all of the team's goals. I became a fast runner, and I wasn't afraid to head the ball, either, even when the coach punted it high up into the air and everyone else would run away. I would always run *toward* the ball and strike it before it could strike me.

And so my dad made up this game where he'd invest one hundred dollars into my portfolio every time I pushed a soccer ball past the opposing goalie and into the net. When I was little, I had no concept of money or the stock market or anything else. But my father went absolutely nuts every time I scored. He'd practically do cartwheels down the sidelines while screaming his head off. It used to make me laugh when I was little because it was so surprising. My father barely ever smiled, let alone whooped and yelled and danced around.

I liked making Dad go wild.

Whenever I scored, we would sit at the computer together later that night, transfer money from his account to mine, and make stock market trades, investing the money I'd earned by scoring goals. I didn't really care about my portfolio, especially since I was never allowed to take out any money to spend, so what was the point? But I liked sitting on my dad's lap and listening to the enthusiastic way he spoke whenever the subject of money came up. Some kids play Candy Land or Chutes and Ladders with their dads, and I played the Dow Jones and Nasdaq. That's just the way it was.

My dad worked a lot, and I mostly saw him—apart from nightly dinner—only at my soccer games or when I was invited into his home office to invest my goal-scoring money. Because I loved my dad, I tried to score as many goals as I could just to keep our relationship alive.

7

It Would Have Been Horrible to Say All This

My family took a few road trips north and south to visit colleges. One thing that bothered me was that my parents scheduled the trips without really asking me whether I even wanted to go to college. It was just assumed that I did. I thought I would actually go to college back then, but their never even asking upset me a little bit nonetheless.

I talked to Booker about this in his living room, on his itchy plaid couch that looked as if it were made out of old-man pants, and he said, "The fight's on, sister. It all starts now. You have to make some real-life choices."

"What choices?" I asked.

"What type of person are you going to be?"

"What types are there?"

"Don't play dumb with me. You know very well that there are two types."

"I have no idea what you're talking about."

"Well, there's the type of person who says there are certain types of people and then tries to be one type or the other. And then there are others who say bananas to the whole concept of types and won't allow themselves to be filed neatly away under some sort of ridiculously limiting category."

"What type are you?" I asked.

"Oh, I don't believe in types."

"But you just said there are two types!"

"Those who believe in types and those who don't."

"You're making my head hurt!"

"Bananas!"

"What?" I said, and then laughed.

"The point, Young Nanette, is not to wear a type like a set of prison shackles."

Later, as I sat in the leather backseat of my mom's Mercedes-Benz SUV on my way to my first "unofficial" college visit, I kept feeling as though I were actually shackled—like I was being carted off to market. These universities wanted my feet and my lungs and my thighs and my shins and my stomach and my forehead, and they wanted me to sweat for them and chase a ball around on a grass field and do whatever it took to get it into a net. It seemed sort of barbaric when I broke it down like that. There was an auction going on. My goal-scoring body was up for sale.

In the front seat, my parents talked a lot about my future—all the possible majors I could choose; the places I would travel if I played soccer for this or that college team, some of which even scheduled internationally in Europe and South America; and the lifelong benefits of belonging to certain alumni associations.

I kept getting mad at myself because I realized that there were many kids my age around the world who didn't have enough food to eat or access to clean drinking water, and here I was, feeling imprisoned in a fifty-thousand-dollar luxury car en route to top universities that wanted to educate me for free.

Comparing myself to a slave.

Seriously?

I kept berating myself for being ungrateful, and yet I couldn't shake the feeling that it was a trick somehow.

I knew I was privileged, but what good was that if I still didn't get to make my own choices? Was it a privilege to be secretly miserable my entire life?

And when we were at the universities meeting with admissions officers and soccer coaches and players, I mostly kept quiet and observed my parents as they chatted with everyone about me as if I weren't even in the room. Sometimes they'd say, "Isn't that right, Nanette?" and I could tell they wanted me to speak more and pretend that I actually wanted to chitchat with all these strangers. But I didn't find the landscaping as beautiful as my parents did, nor did I see the "storied history in the buildings." Nor did I find the list of classes as intellectually stimulating, or the coaches' philosophies as impressive, or the potential teammates as congenial as Mom and Dad did. And yet I knew it would have been horrible to say all this, so I said nothing. Instead, I smiled and nodded until the muscles in my face and neck cramped.

My parents kept asking me what I thought and I kept stalling, saying, "I don't know. There's so much to consider."

"Well," my father said in the car once our college tour was concluded, "after visiting five schools that all but promised you academic and athletic scholarships next year, I really don't think you can make a bad choice."

"I envy you," Mom said.

So I just stared out the window and bit down on my tongue until it started to bleed.

8

Speeding Up the Process a Bit

Out of the blue one day, the first week of August, just before my senior year began, Booker told me he knew another teacher at another high school about a half hour's drive away. "Just one more lonely kid who read my book at the right time, wrote to me, and then became an English teacher."

I asked him if he had fans teaching at every high school in America.

He smiled. "There are a lot of lonely kids in this world, but the problem is that they don't know about each other. If the lonely kids could just team up, a lot of good things would happen, but the world is incredibly afraid of lonely people teaming up, and so it does its best to keep them apart."

"Why?"

"Because lonely people often have great ideas but no support. People with support too often have bad ideas but power. And you don't give up power. No one does, regardless of whether they have good ideas or not. No one gives up power without a long, bloody fight—one that usually involves foul play. Lonely people typically can't stomach treachery, and that's another problem. They tend to tell the truth and fight fair. So we need art and music and poetry for the lonely people to rally around." Booker looked at me for a moment, smiled knowingly, and then said, "I think you should meet this kid who's been sending me poetry. I like his words. You two would get along. He calls himself Little Lex. He was a student of the teacher I just mentioned. She gave him a copy of my book, just like Jared Graves gave it to you. He also became obsessed with Wrigley. So you already have that in common."

"Are you setting me up? I've never dated anyone before, you know."

"He's a talented poet. Reminds me of you."

"How so? I'm not a poet."

"Well, I like *him* a lot. I like *you* a lot. Do the math!"

"What does he look like?"

"Does it matter?"

"Of course!"

"Well then, let me see. He has three heads, seven eyes, one nose, two forked tongues, scales all over his body, a tail, and—"

"Seriously."

"I don't know. I've never seen him in person. He doesn't send me pictures. But he's coming for dinner this Saturday night, and so are you. I've told him all about my Nanette, and I have a feeling you might end up marrying each other and making future babies."

"Stop it! I can't believe you're setting me up on a blind date!"

"It's dinner. Don't be so dramatic. We're going to eat. Drink coffee. Talk about the weather. Maybe he'll read you one of his poems. That's not going to kill anyone, is it? Why label the event as a date? Why can't it just be a discussion among three people?"

But when I arrived at Booker's that Saturday night, I immediately realized I had absolutely been tricked into going on a blind date. Candles flickered on the dining room table, scratchy classical music spun out of an antique record player that looked decades older than me, and an arrangement of chocolate-covered strawberries served as the centerpiece. A very large boy with enormous hands and shoulder-length blond hair was seated at the head of the table, and he kept cracking his knuckles, which made me trust him for some reason.

Booker put his arm around me and said, "Nanette, this is Little Lex. Little Lex, this is Nanette. Speak amongst yourselves as I prepare our feast."

When Booker left, Little Lex said "Hey" from behind a curtain of hair.

I sat down.

"I don't know what Booker told you, but—"

"Don't worry," he said. "I know I'm out of my league here."

41

"What do you mean?"

He shrugged and then looked out the window.

"You like the Buk?" I asked, and pointed to Lex's T-shirt, on which Charles Bukowski's almost-werewolf-like head screamed in black and white over a plastic cup of bloodred wine.

He looked down at the old poet's face and said, "Love him."

"You've been sending Booker your own poetry?"

"Yeah."

"Nice. So then you're an official poet?"

"Booker has me trying to avoid labels."

"Me too."

I looked around the room for a few moments and heard Little Lex tapping his black Chuck Taylor sneaker too rapidly.

"You read *The Bubblegum Reaper*, right?" I said.

"Of course."

"Lena Thatch."

"What about her?"

"You're tapping your foot like she does. When she's in the cafeteria and Wrigley is watching her. Wrigley's true love. It's Lena, right?"

"Could be Stella," Little Lex said, meeting my eyes for the first time.

"Why do you say that?"

"Well, here's the thing," he said, and then told me a few of his theories.

We talked about *The Bubblegum Reaper* for a good half hour, and I soon learned that Little Lex had memorized all the same quotes that I had and that he had been having the exact same experience with Booker's novel—only his sophomore-year English teacher had given him a photocopied version and not a real paperback, and he thought Stella was Wrigley's true love and I believed in Lena. Somewhere during the conversation, I discovered that I was enjoying myself immensely, that time was flying by like pelicans over the sea while you stretch out on a towel during a hot summer's day. I had had access to the wonderful, amazing world of *The Bubblegum Reaper* for the past eight months but no one to share it with because I didn't know anyone else who had read my favorite novel except Booker, who had forbidden me to speak about it, and Mr. Graves, who was officially gone. Sharing it with Little Lex now was a way to experience it for the first time again—through another's eyes.

"When I first read the ending," Little Lex said, "and Wrigley says he understands Unproductive Ted and that he's quitting, when Wrigley's floating in the creek—that's when everything clicked into place in my mind."

"What do you mean?" I said.

"I realized I could quit."

"Quit what?"

Right then, Booker came in with a large bowl of spaghetti, mushrooms, and spinach. "*Italiano!*" he said in a funny accent, and then began to scoop his creation onto our plates. When he was finished, Booker sat and said, "I think I may have heard talk of a certain book that has been banned in this house."

Little Lex and I glanced at each other.

"Enough of that," Booker said. "Little Lex, why don't you read us some of your radical, life-altering, vivid poetry?"

"Now?" he said as his face went red.

"Oh, he's just being modest," Booker said to me. "After all, he brought his briefcase with him, and I'm pretty sure it's full of poems. He simply cannot wait any longer. The poet must sing!"

"You *made* me bring my poems. You said you wouldn't let me in without them!" Little Lex said.

"Wouldn't you like to hear a sample of Little Lex's poetry, Nanette?"

"I would," I said. "But please don't feel obligated."

"I'll make her a copy after dinner, and she can read it later. Is that okay?" he said to Booker.

"It's *your* poetry," Booker said. "No one can tell you what to do with your own art unless you let them."

"Is your teacher still teaching?" I asked Lex, trying to change the subject because I was beginning to feel sorry for him. Booker was obviously pushing all of us into situations we weren't ready for.

"Which teacher?"

"The one who gave you my book, she means," Booker said.

"Yeah. She is."

"Lucky you," I said.

"The teacher who gave you the book we shall not name isn't?" Lex asked.

"Nope. I scared him away," I said, surprising myself.

"What did you do?"

"I don't know," I lied, suddenly realizing what an uncomfortable conversational road I was going down. When Lex squinted at me and cocked his head to the right, I added, "I was just kidding."

"How's the food?" Booker asked, changing the subject once more, only for my benefit.

Little Lex and I both raved about the meal, even though it was cold and tasteless. We pushed it around on the plates a little and ate all of the warm, heavily buttered crusty bread, and then suddenly Booker was washing dishes in the kitchen and Lex and I had little cups of espresso in front of us, and the lights had been dimmed and the chocolate-covered strawberries were in our bellies.

"So you hang out with Booker all the time?" Little Lex asked.

"He's sort of like the grandfather I never had. Well, I actually have two grandfathers, but I never see them. What about you and Booker?"

"He's been writing me these letters. I have a hundred and four in a shoe box at home. Put them all together and you have enough words for another Booker novel. Although I've been forbidden to show anyone what he's written, of course. He actually said I'd 'die a slow, painful death if I ever break my solemn vow.' I'm pretty sure he's serious, because he's sent me pictures of his secret samurai sword collection."

We both laughed, and then Little Lex said, "My teacher gave me *The Bubblegum Reaper* after some bad stuff happened."

I made a note to ask what happened to Lex but let him continue. The caffeine had him talking more and with great speed.

"When I came in raving about the read, she told me to write Booker a fan letter, and then somehow Booker and I were writing almost weekly." He looked over at the kitchen doorway, lowered his voice, and said, "I was sort of worried at first, like maybe he was after something, because why would he take the time to write a kid like me? Although I couldn't figure out what he could possibly want. Now I think he's just a lonely old man. Maybe he would have started corresponding with anyone who wrote a fan letter."

I lowered my voice, too, and said, "He *is* lonely. But I don't think he would write many people, actually. I think he only interacts with people who are like Wrigley and whichever Thatch twin talks to turtles."

"Maybe."

Little Lex was a big, heavyset guy with hunched shoulders, but somehow he carried his weight well, and he had thick, rich hair and bright eyes and a kind smile. What I liked most about him was that he didn't seem to be trying to prove anything at all—no pretense.

"So why *do* they call you Little Lex?" I asked in my regular speaking voice, thinking I knew the answer.

He scrunched up his face like he had just tasted something sour. "It's not a very happy story."

"So."

"You really want to know?"

When I nodded, he reached down into his leather briefcase and pulled out a worn notebook and some tracing paper. Next, he furiously traced something—his pencil dancing with great speed for several minutes, his brow wrinkling and unwrinkling—while I watched and wondered. Then he folded the sheet of tracing paper up into a small square and slid it toward me.

"A poem?" I said.

"Yeah. Don't read it in front of me, okay? Not even Booker has read this one. He wanted me to read poetry to you tonight. But I—I just can't."

I picked up the folded piece of paper, stuck it in my pocket, and said, "So why do you think Booker set us up like this?"

"I don't know. I didn't ask him to. I just wanted to meet him after writing so many letters."

"So this is really, truly the first time you've met him?"

"Yeah. I tried before, but Booker used to say our friendship was 'pure' because it was all through words and that meeting face-to-face would mean risking it all, which made me want to meet him even more. Also, I just got my driver's license and a car. So this was the first time I could visit without asking for a ride from my dad. And Booker doesn't drive, as you know."

"Why didn't you want to ask your dad for a ride?"

"I guess I just want to keep my worlds separate."

I nodded because I knew exactly what he meant. Spending time with Booker was becoming an addiction, mostly because it was the only part of my day when I felt like I could be myself—or maybe like there was one person in the world who didn't want me to become something I didn't want to be or to act a certain way or to go along with everything that others pushed into my life. I kept my parents away from Booker, too, because I was afraid they'd infect him with their ideas for my future—their vision for who I should be. Half the time I spent with Booker, my parents thought I was hanging out with my teammates.

I said, "Do you think it's weird that Booker tricked us into going on a blind date and yet neither of us seems mad or upset? I'm not upset. Are you? I mean, you could be pretending. But you seem pretty okay with tonight."

He blinked a few times as if he was surprised by my words, and then the sentences that came out of his mouth were both wonderful and sad. "Honestly? This is the best night I've had in years. Maybe in my entire lifetime."

"Seriously?"

He nodded a bit too eagerly, and I could see the little-kid face still hidden behind his long hair and stubble beard, but it was cute, and I suddenly realized that maybe it was the best night I'd had in years, too.

We talked some more over our espressos before we "retired" to Booker's sunroom for a game of Scrabble, which Booker won by thirty or so points, playing the word *qi* on a triple-word score, trash-talking the whole time, but Little Lex and I didn't really mind losing.

When the game was over, Booker and I walked Lex to his car—a brand-new Jeep Wrangler Unlimited with a soft top—and said an awkward good-bye, especially because Booker said, "No kissing my girl on the first date! I've got a shotgun inside! I'll put a bowling-ball-sized hole in your stomach if you don't treat her right!"

All the blood drained from Little Lex's face—not because he thought Booker would ever be violent, but because our hero was bringing up our teenage lust before we had properly dealt with it ourselves—and then Lex just drove away without saying anything else.

"What are you up to?" I asked Booker. "Why did you humiliate us like that?"

"Just speeding up the process a bit for you. You won't be young forever! You should read Philip Larkin's poem "Annus Mirabilis." You'll thank me someday."

"What?"

"And when you read that poem in your pocket, you're going to be head over heels. The kid has talent and quite an impressive heart, too."

"Were you eavesdropping the entire time you were in the kitchen?"

"Of course!"

"You're a crazy old man."

"That's the best kind to be!"

That night, in my perfectly-decorated-by-my-mother bedroom, where I am not permitted to hang a single thing on the pistachio-green walls, I opened up the folded tracing paper.

9

Just to Get Rid of the Cannonballs

LITTLE LEX

By Alex Redmer

"Call him LITTLE," one of them said,
_   "because he is not"_
So they started calling him LITTLE Lex
He was fat and round and short and scared
Like a meteorite that had fallen from the sky
Wondering where he had landed and why
But never getting an answer as he cooled
And he winced when they called him LITTLE
And he puked in the locker room stall after
They stole his shirt and rattail-whipped him
_   with theirs_

And then he was punished
Because he was late for class
Because he had no shirt
For not being LITTLE
And he asked his father why
But his father didn't know
And his teachers didn't seem to care
Because they rewarded the ones who invented
Cruel names for the ones the teachers never
    rewarded
And it went on like this
It went on and it went on and on and on and on
But then Little Lex grew tall like an oak tree,
Or a rocket ship
And he was no longer round but rectangular
And his hands were heavy as cannonballs
And his fists could knock the lights out
Of the name-callers' eyes, which happened
More than once
Easy as snuffing a candle
After licking your fingers
There was blood
And then there were lawyers
And the school principal held a meeting
And everyone agreed
The name LITTLE Lex
Would be banned
Along with his cannonball hands

So the boy named himself LITTLE Lex
And refused to be called by any other moniker
Even when they didn't want to call
Him LITTLE
He made them
The teachers
The parents
The principal
Everyone
He said, "Call me LITTLE now or else!"
And they did
Just to get rid of the cannonballs
To keep the blood where it belonged
In the name-callers' bodies
And he was glad to have a choice
And he was
No longer afraid
And no one stole his shirt
Or poked his soft belly with a bony finger
Or punished him unfairly
Or laughed at him when they called him LITTLE
But he was lonely
If only a little
Because he missed the old Alex
—JUST PLAIN ALEX
Who had never hurt anybody

10

Let's Plug Our Phones In and Sleep Together

Little Lex had written his e-mail address at the bottom of the poem, along with his cell phone number.

We were texting back and forth five minutes after I finished reading "LITTLE Lex," and then we were FaceTiming on our iPhones, both of our heads under the covers, which were illuminated by the screens like flashlights in tents.

We talked about his poem.

We talked about *The Bubblegum Reaper*.

We talked about Booker.

We even talked about our parents and kids in our schools and how we both sort of felt lost—and it was wonderful to be so honest with someone my own age, someone who also knew "the great invisible solitary" that Booker talks about in his novel.

I mentioned Philip Larkin's poem "Annus Mirabilis," and Lex said, "The title's Latin for 'year of wonders.'"

"How do you know that? Do you take Latin?"

"No. I looked it up when I first read the poem. Want me to read it to you? I have the book right here."

He read it in this very serious voice.

It's about sex.

When he finished, we were completely silent for too long, so we laughed to clear the awkward.

Because it's mentioned in the poem, we Googled *the Chatterley ban* and learned about D. H. Lawrence and the controversy surrounding his book *Lady Chatterley's Lover*, which was apparently outlawed for being pornographic even though the synopsis sounded incredibly boring by today's standards. Some websites say it's about how you can't truly be alive without having vivid sexual experiences. Others say it's sexist or a male fantasy.

"Why would Booker tell you to read *that* poem?" Little Lex said.

"Maybe because it's about more than sex. It's about time, I think. And timing. And missing out on good things because of others' beliefs."

And then we talked about *The Bubblegum Reaper* some more and how Booker maybe was playing a role for us, because deep down inside that old man lived a sadness that paired well with the Larkin poem.

At some point during that first FaceTime conversation, I started to call my new friend Alex instead of Little Lex, and he didn't correct me, which felt significant after reading the poem he traced.

Alex read me more Philip Larkin poems from the collection Booker had sent him in the mail as a present, and it was then that I realized the old man knew that Alex and I would be having a postdate talk and had planted "Annus Mirabilis" in my mind so that we would have a good discussion topic. Booker knew I'd look up and read anything he referenced or recommended, and so it felt as if the old man was playing some sort of chess match with young love and we were the pieces and Booker was winning.

We talked a lot about a poem called "High Windows," which Alex read to me. At first I thought it, too, was about sex, but really it's about how maybe there isn't anything above us at all when we look up through a high window—and so maybe there is no god, no nothing, which sounds depressing, but Larkin makes it okay and even beautiful, which is sort of a relief.

"Do you believe in God?" I asked Alex.

"I don't know. Do you?"

"I don't know, either."

And then we talked about God for a long time—making a list of all the things that make you want to believe in God, like sunsets and lilies and chai tea with frothy steamed milk, and indie music and wild anonymous acts of charity and books and movies and poetry. But then we talked about all the things that make you give up on the idea of a god, like war and poverty and disease and psychopaths who shoot up people in movie theaters or malls, and friends who let you down and turn mean as they get older, and acne and the need for bathrooms, and stomaching the absurdity of a public school education—although Alex said he went to a private prep elementary school, and it had been even worse. "They taught us that we were better than everyone who wasn't enrolled at our school, and we believed that. It was ugly." When we were being honest, it was easier to fill the "No God" list, even though I got the feeling that we both didn't want it to be that way.

Booker had told Alex about Charles Bukowski, too, and so we took turns reading each other Bukowski poems. Alex read me one called "Bluebird," which I hadn't heard before.

It was about hiding something beautiful deep inside you.

I loved it.

"Do you ever weep?" I asked Alex, because Bukowski says he doesn't in the poem.

"Um," he said, looking away from his iPhone camera lens. "*Yes?* I'm no Bukowski, I guess."

For some reason I told him about what happened when I tried to kiss Mr. Graves and how I ended up sobbing in the nurse's office on the bed behind the white curtain. Alex was the first person I told. And to my great surprise, it didn't freak him out. He just listened, and then he said, "I'm sorry that happened to you." And it felt wonderful to get that secret out of me—to know that Alex didn't hate me for telling the truth or think I was a whore or a freak.

Just to make sure, I said, "You must think that I'm a nymphomaniac—trying to kiss my teacher."

"Sounds like you were just confused. I get confused all the time," he said, which made me want to kiss Alex.

Then we talked a lot about our parents and how we didn't want to become them, but we had no other role models—or "maps," Alex kept saying. "My father is a terrible map, mostly because he doesn't ever lead me anywhere." And I thought about my parents being maps that led to places I didn't want to go—and it made a shocking amount of sense, using the word *maps* to describe parents. It almost made you feel like you could fold Mom and Dad up and lock them away in the glove compartment of your car and just joyride for the rest of your life maybe.

Toward the end of our epic phone conversation, Alex and I were just sort of lying there, looking at each other's faces through the screens on our little machines, which sounds weird now but felt right—like we were both tired of being alone and therefore didn't want to say good-bye.

Alex had a wonderful face.

I studied it pixel by pixel.

I could have looked at it forever.

"Let's plug our phones in and sleep together," he said. "We don't have to say good-bye."

"Okay."

And so we drifted off to sleep without shutting off our phones, and it felt nice and safe to have him there with me.

When I woke up the next morning and looked at the screen, it was blank. Must have shut off in the middle of the night. I wanted to call him immediately to continue whatever it was we had started. And then it hit me: For the first time, I felt like I knew why girls so often lose their minds when they were in lust or love and how Shannon could get pregnant and how my parents came together so many years ago.

Love and lust were a madness that threatened everything, and yet, if you were in heat, you did not care.

11

The Sexual Tendencies of Teenage Boys

I met Shannon at the Rainbow Dragons' first soccer practice. Our parents had signed us up. I was standing off to the side, waiting for whatever was about to happen, and this small girl with long, shiny black hair walked over to me, grabbed my hand, and pulled me into the flock of girls waiting for the balls to be released from the coach's net bag.

"My name is Shannon Welsh. Let's be friends," she said, and I nodded.

Shortly after that, Shannon's picking me out seemed sort of fated, because she would go on to develop the best cross on the team. She was one of the first girls who could actually lift the ball into the air and send it with any accuracy, so our coaches quickly paired us as a team within a team.

The strategy for much of our early days was to get the ball to Shannon by sending it past the defenders and toward the flag (or the other team's corner), and then Shannon would outrun the defender while I ran toward the goal. She would cross the ball to my head or foot, and I would score. We did this hundreds of times, all throughout town soccer and then on the traveling teams and finally on our high school's varsity team, which we both made as freshmen.

Shannon has often said that I am her best friend, although I have never formally agreed to take the job. Unlike me, Shannon is as girly as they come, constantly experimenting with makeup, different hairstyles, and tanning products. She's beautiful off the field, but she's *most* beautiful on the field, with her hair pulled back into a simple ponytail and her jersey soaked with sweat, and minimal makeup—only she doesn't believe it.

I always knew Shannon and I were different. She was very talkative in groups and I wasn't. She was the first girl in our class to have a boyfriend, and that happened when we were in third grade. She even made me her maid of honor in a pretend back-yard wedding, which felt as though someone had stuck live electrical wires under my skin, although I did not protest.

And by the time we were in the seventh grade, Shannon was performing fellatio on older high school boys who only seemed to come around when they wanted blow jobs. She'd tell me all about it in great detail, almost as if she were trying to make me jealous or prove to herself that she really enjoyed it, when all the while it was painfully obvious that she was being used.

The worst part was that she knew she was being used and *everyone* knew the boys were complete assholes, but Shannon claimed to love the sex. And maybe she *did* love it—not just the attention from older boys and the alcohol they gave her as thanks, but the actual feeling of sex. And if I'm being honest, maybe it's why I tried to kiss my English teacher, too. It felt *good*.

Regardless, the older boys told their friends about how easy it was to get middle school girls to give head and then all the high school boys were cruising past our middle school on a daily basis, asking if we car-less girls needed rides home and maybe would like something to drink. Shannon and many of the Rainbow Dragons got into those cars until the parents figured out what was going on and someone's father got a lawyer involved.

My mother asked me if I ever got into "one of those boy party cars that were cruising by your school looking for BJs," and when I told her I hadn't, she asked me why not, which confused me.

"Shannon's mother called. Your best friend was a regular, apparently. But she said you never went. Why?"

"Did you *want* me to go?"

"Of course not."

"So why would you ask me that?"

Mom looked at me for a long time and then said, "Do you like boys?"

"What?" I said, even though I realized my mother was asking me if I were a lesbian.

"It's okay if you don't. I just wanted to—"

"Can we *not* talk about this?"

"Fine," Mom said, and then stormed out of the room like I had offended her. And I've thought for years about that conversation and what it meant. She never said she was proud of me for not going with the older boys, nor did she say she thought any less of Shannon, who was a regular at our home and clearly one of Mom's favorites—they used to talk a lot about beauty tips. And then I realized that not going along with the crowd—even when it meant not performing oral sex on older boys—could make you seem odd or weird.

My dad never said a word to me about what my friends were jokingly calling our "middle school sex scandal."

But, of course, Shannon asked me why I never went along with them. It was maybe a month or so after the parents put an end to the sex rides. We were in her room and she was halfway through one of the many small bottles of peach schnapps her high school hookups had given her in exchange for blow jobs.

"Do you really think you're better than us?" she said, a little tipsy, and then laughed. "Just because you've never had any fun with a boy? Or is it that you just don't like boys?"

"I don't want to talk about it, okay?"

"*Okay.*"

The lesbian rumors began the next day in school—boys coughing into their hands and then quickly saying, "*Um, dyke.*"

It was all so ridiculous and more than a little depressing.

The funny thing was that I absolutely knew Shannon had started those rumors, or at least she didn't defend me, because she was popular enough to make them stop, but I kept pretending that Shannon and I were friends anyway. She did the same. She racked up assists on the soccer field. I scored a lot of goals. Our coaches and parents said we were the perfect team, and so I tried not to do anything to upset our "on-field chemistry." And all the adults in our lives pretended not to notice that Shannon was routinely drunk and having sexual experiences with a different boy every so many weeks. To be fair, many of the kids in my middle school were doing the same exact thing. Who knows? Maybe giving blow jobs is a natural rite of passage that can be a wonderfully rewarding extracurricular activity, and I was missing out—I was one of the weird ones.

But it wasn't even about the sex. I had nothing against sex. I wanted to experience it just like everyone else. What I initially resisted was the crowd mentality of it. Blow older boys because everyone else is. Drink because everyone else is. If it had been "ride a live two-hump camel to school because everyone else is," I still would have resisted because I don't want to be like everyone else. And I love riding camels! Shannon hates riding camels. I know because we rode them at the zoo when we were in second grade. There is a funny pic. Me waving and smiling in between two humps as Shannon screams and cries on a camel behind me. And if I'm being truthful, there was a part of me, even as a little kid, that enjoyed the camel ride simply because Shannon didn't. I was so tired of doing everything she liked that it felt redemptive to be doing something she hated, or, more accurately, *not doing* something she loved.

"You should go to more parties, Nanette," Mom would say

when I stayed in and read on the weekends. "You need to be more social. Like Shannon."

The lesbian rumors suddenly stopped when we started high school, and I'm pretty sure that Shannon had something to do with that, too, because it was the year her mother came out as a lesbian and left her father. Shannon and her mother moved across town and in with a woman lawyer whom Shannon's mom met, ironically, via "the middle school sex scandal." Around this time, Shannon stopped going to parties and spent a lot of time in my room crying and telling me all her secrets—such as which boys she'd blown versus which she had actually fucked. I mostly listened because I thought that was the right thing to do.

Regardless, she earned more assists and I scored more goals, and our varsity team won a lot of games, and my father cheered like a madman on the sidelines and my stock portfolio grew.

After I kissed Mr. Graves and he stopped meeting me during lunch periods, Shannon kept asking me what was wrong, saying I was clearly depressed. There were a few times I was actually tempted to tell her the truth, but then I would remember all the homophobic comments I had to endure during our middle school years, and I'd juxtapose those with the fact that Shannon was now the president of the Gay-Straight Alliance in our high school, of which I was also a proud member, representing the straights, and somehow I knew better than to let Shannon see any real part of me.

Shannon got pregnant during our junior year.

She wasn't even sure whose kid it was, so she didn't tell any of the boys she had slept with. According to our math, there were three candidates. I know, because I was the only person she told about her pregnancy, and she told me *everything*. Her last period had been at least eight weeks before, and she'd been secretly terrified for almost two months. She cried ferociously when she told me. We stayed up all night one weekend making a pros-and-cons chart so she could decide whether to have an abortion. By morning, she had decided that she would indeed "terminate the pregnancy," and so we went to the kitchen and showed her two moms the pregnancy tests.

Shannon's biological mom completely lost her mind, only she didn't yell at Shannon for being pregnant, but for "allowing" it to happen.

Shannon's stepmom, Joyce, was calmer about it and pleaded with Shannon's real mom, saying, "They even made a pros-and-cons chart. How many kids would do that in an effort to prepare for this conversation?"

Shannon was sobbing by this point, and I was staring at my hands.

I went to the abortion clinic with Shannon and her moms, only to find out that Shannon somehow had a "silent miscarriage" and didn't know it—apparently, a tiny baby's heart can just stop beating—which everyone agreed was "a blessing," so we went out for an expensive dinner in the city, a French place called Parc, and then we never talked about what had happened ever again.

My friend went on the Pill and kept saying I should be on it, too, even though I wasn't sexually active.

The funny thing was that we all had to sign a contract at the beginning of every sports season that said we would not drink alcohol, do drugs, or use tobacco products, and yet almost all athletes at our high school broke that contract weekly and made fun of me for taking it seriously, because they didn't know about the mimosas I had with Mom on Sunday mornings.

My father once told me that he drank beer in high school, and then he added, "There's nothing wrong with a beer or two. Just stay away from liquor, okay?" And I knew that he was giving me permission to drink, but I didn't anyway. I didn't really want to drink, and I didn't like going to the parties where Shannon would get so drunk that she could hardly stand and would end up having sex in the bed of someone's parents.

I found it all so very depressing.

I used to try to talk to Mr. Graves about it and he would say, "I don't want to know," and then cover his ears, which was when I realized that there was nothing he could do about it. He had to pretend that his students were really smart, conscientious kids destined to be the type of adults who would make a positive difference in the world—his belief in the power of teaching required this—and I started to understand that it was hard for a teacher to spend the entire weekend grading essays and lesson planning for a bunch of sex-crazed, alcoholic kids.

"Do you know what most sex-crazed, alcoholic kids grow up to be?" Booker once said to me. "Their sex-crazed, alcoholic parents."

And I thought about how everyone knew that Shannon's dad was always at the local bar drinking and, according to my parents, "hitting on anything and everything with boobs." He had become sort of notorious after Shannon's mom left him for a woman. It was almost as if he was trying to prove his manhood or something. And Shannon's two moms drank a lot of wine, too. There was always at least one open bottle and glasses poured whenever I visited Shannon's home. I assumed Carol and Joyce probably hooked up while Shannon's biological parents were still married.

I got this crazy idea that maybe if I refrained from sex and drinking—maybe it would mean that my parents weren't sex-crazed alcoholics.

Maybe they would remain married and be happy.

Maybe my mom wouldn't hate the way my father chewed his food, and maybe my dad would put his arm around Mom again the way he did when I was little.

I knew it was an inane thing to believe, but it helped.

It was something I could do.

And it wasn't even hard—until I met Alex.

Ironically, Alex didn't seem all that interested in sex. I had been to enough parties sober to know the sexual tendencies of teenage boys—the way they would try to rush things along the same way they would bang on the bathroom doors when their bladders were full of beer and say, "Come on, I really need to go!" as if we girls might be filing our nails in there or maybe just reading a book. I'd watched them lean in too close during conversations. I'd watched their hands casually land on the thighs of my teammates, and I'd watched my teammates pretend not to notice. I'd even seen boys adjust their genitalia in the middle of conversations with my teammates because the boys were aroused, and I'd watched my teammates pretend not to notice, even though they all talked about the boys' dicks in great detail when the fellas weren't around. And I had never been interested in any of it.

I used to worry that I was asexual or something, but as Alex and I got to know each other, taking long rides in his Jeep with the top down, going to art house movies, reading each other poetry on park benches in the city, I started to realize what sexual attraction was all about. I found myself glancing at different parts of Alex's body and wanting to explore—not because all the other girls on my team already had, but because it all suddenly felt so right, natural, real. And I also started to worry because Alex *wasn't* putting his hand on my thigh or leaning in too close or grabbing me. He just listened to everything I had to say, and I could tell he was really interested, which made me worry he didn't think I was pretty. That was a new fear for me. Suddenly, I wanted to be attractive, adored, desired.

12

Dozens of Deadly Laser Beams

"I want to quit soccer," I told Booker as we were sitting on his backyard bench next to Don Quixote and his windmills. We were drinking ice-cold glasses of freshly squeezed lemonade garnished with mint leaves picked from Booker's garden. "I really don't want to play my senior-year season."

"I can't have this conversation again. If you haven't quit by now, you never will. You've been thoroughly brainwashed by the soccer community."

It was true that I had told him I would quit all through winter indoor and then after spring soccer and then after the summer sessions with the young semipro trainers from England who always ended up at our parties and sleeping with my teammates, who all fell in love with their accents. But that was all before Alex.

"I'm going to quit tomorrow. I'm calling Coach and telling him I'm done," I said rather defiantly, but I didn't do it.

It was a speech by Shannon that finally pushed me to the breaking point, on a blazing-hot August day, the first official practice of our senior year. Coach Miller had run us hard through conditioning—full-speed dribbling and passing sprints; long, seemingly endless attacking and defending drills; and my least favorite, where he made squares out of cones and you had to play keep-away for twenty minutes, and if anyone stopped moving for even a few seconds, the whole team had to sprint a mile and start over. Coach always caught at least one person, and we had to sprint two miles that day before we got our full twenty minutes. The whole practice, I kept thinking about Alex and how I would much rather be somewhere alone with him, expressing myself and discussing literature, than conditioning with girls I didn't really like or understand, all in an effort to kick a ball into a net more times than girls from other schools did.

At the end of each practice, we'd sit between the goalposts and Coach would give us a talk before he allowed the captains to take over, at which point Shannon and I were expected to give motivational speeches and address any concerns that other girls didn't feel comfortable bringing up directly to Coach. Shannon always assumed that leader role very easily, which was almost comical, because anywhere else in her life—when she was not addressing shin-pad-wearing girls in a soccer goal—she was prone to follow boys with seedy plans for her. And I wondered if she was just following Coach's plans for her the same way she got into those cars full of high school boys back when we were in middle school. Maybe Shannon would do whatever an older man told her to do.

"Your goal this year, ladies," Shannon said, waving her index finger over the entire team, "is to win a state championship. Anything less than that is a failure. But if we bring the state title home this year, you'll have that for the rest of your lives. No one will be able to take it away from you. No matter what else happens or doesn't happen from then on, you'll always be a champion. Forever."

It was the same pep talk bullshit we had been hearing and parroting since we were little kids playing for the Rainbow Dragons, but maybe it was also like eating one too many bites of food, because suddenly I felt like I was going to vomit.

"We have the talent and the dedication and—hey, Nanette, where're you going?" Shannon said.

"I'm quitting like a motherfucking champion!"

"What?"

All my teammates laughed, maybe because they were so surprised that I used the word *motherfucking* as an adjective. I hardly ever cursed. But cursing suddenly felt good, and so I yelled it once more, even louder.

"I'm a motherfucking champion!"

This time no one laughed.

As I walked across the field, I could feel my teammates' eyes on me—dozens of deadly laser beams searing into my back; I didn't dare turn around.

I held up two middle fingers over my head—something I had never before done in my entire life—and it felt like I was finally free.

My coach came running after me. "What's wrong, Nan?" he said. "What's going on here?"

"My name is Nanette," I said, surprising myself. He had been calling me Nan for almost four years, and I hated it. It felt like he was making fun of my name, the way he said it. Always dragging out the syllable, like he thought it was stupid, maybe because I was the only Nanette he had ever met, so he chopped my name in half to punish me for being unique. "I quit," I said. "I'm done running around after a ball. You can't make me do it anymore. No one can! *I'm already a motherfucking champion!* A champion of myself."

"Whoa. Slow down. What happened?" he said, completely ignoring the swearing I was doing.

"I just don't want to play anymore. I hate soccer. There. I said it. *Finally.*"

"Do you need to talk to Ms. Train?" he said, which was code for *Do you have your period?* Ms. Train was the assistant coach, only she didn't know anything about soccer. She was there to deal with "woman problems." Here I was, telling the truth for the first time, and he wanted to erase it—make it not count—with my menstrual cycle.

"No," I said, and then added, "Fuck soccer."

That night, Coach came to my home, and we all had a sit-down talk.

"Where did this come from?" my dad asked. "You don't mention anything, and then suddenly out of nowhere, you just start cursing and quitting?"

I thought about how this wouldn't surprise the two people who knew me best—Booker and Alex. Even Mr. Graves wouldn't have been surprised, and I hadn't spoken with him in months. But my mom and dad, the people with whom I lived, were shocked.

My father and Coach talked a lot about how many goals I had scored and how I could break the conference scoring record this year, having already broken the school record as a junior, and how colleges would surely invite me on "official" recruiting trips to offer me full scholarships, and it was like they were arguing for me not to kill myself, the way they were talking, as if I were doomed to a shitty life if I stopped playing soccer. Like I wouldn't count as a human being if I stopped scoring goals for teams.

"Her grades are good enough to get her into the best colleges without soccer," Mom finally said. Mom was a cheerleader in high school, and I always got the sense that she didn't think girls should do anything athletic but cheer, so her being on my side was depressing. Also, the smile on her face let me know that she was sort of messing with my dad in front of Coach—like she was attacking his manhood.

"That's really not the point here," Dad shot back at Mom, which was when I realized that my relationship with my father was about to turn for the worse and Mom was trying to form an alliance. By not playing soccer, I was severing the one real connection Dad and I had, and maybe that was why my father was so upset.

(Later, Booker would say, "Well, you weren't going to play organized soccer for the rest of your life, so this moment with your father was imminent. You can't live for someone else. At some point you just explode, which is probably why you began spouting curse words like a Roman candle." At least he understood.)

"You made a commitment to your teammates," Coach said,

pointing his index finger at my face from the stylish comfort of my parents' white leather couch. "You made a commitment to me. You signed a contract."

"You know that every girl on the team violates the no-drinking clause. Are you headed to their houses next to give them the same lecture? I can tell you the names of my teammates who drank with the English soccer coaches you hired to train us—it was all of them except me!" I said, surprising myself again. I had never talked to Coach like that before. "But you already know that! So don't talk to me about fucking contracts!"

Coach looked at my parents for support, and my dad dutifully said, "Don't talk to your coach like that, Nanette. There's no need for swearing."

"Why don't I let you sort this out as a family," Coach said to my parents. He looked pale, like he was starting to fear me. "See you at practice tomorrow, Nanette."

It was the first time he ever used my real name, and it was a moment for me. He respected my wishes because I had something he wanted but wouldn't give up easily, and that was the only reason why. I had asked him to call me Nanette many times during my freshman year when I was competing for a varsity position, but he'd completely ignored me. I suddenly felt an unfamiliar sense of power.

"No, you won't," I said. "I quit."

Coach shook his head and then retreated.

Dad said, "Why are you doing this?"

"She doesn't like playing soccer," Mom said. "Simple as that. It's just a game."

"A game that could pay for her college education."

"We have a college fund for her. We're not exactly poor."

"That's not the point!"

"She was playing for you, Don. But she's not a little girl anymore."

"Sports make women out of girls. Statistically speaking, girls who play varsity sports are more likely to—"

"Please," Mom said. "Like that's the reason you want her to play."

My parents argued like that for a time, and at some point I got up and went to my bedroom. I'm not sure they noticed.

Shannon called and yelled at me for making her look bad in front of the team—for "undermining her authority"—calling me a "crazy bitch traitor." She was ranting and raving when I hung up on her. She called back several times and left messages on my voice mail, but I didn't listen to them.

I called Alex and told him that I was not afraid anymore— that I had quit the soccer team.

"They'll try to make you afraid again," he told me. "But you have to stay strong for a little bit before they'll leave you alone. Trust me. I know the drill."

My teammates e-mailed and called, and Shannon visited my bedroom, trying a different tactic—all of them begging me to play "one more season," Shannon saying she needed me to get her assists and lock up her scholarship. "I need a goal-scorer to finish my crosses!" Suddenly, I was no longer a "crazy bitch traitor." But I had made up my mind and didn't return to the field, which felt sort of thrilling—making a choice for myself.

To solidify things, I cut the first day of my senior year and had Alex drive us to the beach.

Cutting was an automatic suspension from the team, and one

of the few rules that was actually enforced. So I called the school secretary and told her I was cutting. "Call my parents. Report me to all the appropriate authority figures. I expect to be punished to the fullest extent of the law. Please let Coach Miller know."

Alex cut his school because I asked him to—I said that I needed him.

I had never needed a boy before, and I wondered if Booker had some type of psychic powers.

Could he see the future?

After an hour's drive, we found a beach that didn't have a lifeguard and therefore wasn't all that crowded.

We swam out into the Atlantic and floated on our backs.

I thought about Unproductive Ted and why he sat alone all day long on his rock.

I was glad to have Alex with me, but I also felt like I could be alone with Alex, too, which was a new feeling—being alone with another person.

I swam over to Alex and kissed him on the lips.

He kissed me back using his tongue.

My first French kiss.

We wrapped our arms around each other, and soon he was hard—I could tell because it was pressing up against my naked stomach below in the sea.

Neither of us said anything about that.

We only kissed.

And I wasn't afraid, like I thought I would be.

When I returned to school the next day, none of my teammates looked at me—not even Shannon. I heard a few kids cough when I walked by and then say "Um—muff diver" really fast. Or "carpet muncher." Or "scissor sister." And I wondered if the head of the Gay-Straight Alliance could be up to her old tricks again. I was exercising my heterosexuality for the first time in my life, but that wasn't something I wanted to share with the idiots who attended my high school. So I wore the lesbian comments like a mask that kept everything I really loved private and safe and beyond the dirty grasp of the people who didn't know the real, true me and never would. And regardless, I had nothing against lesbians. My classmates were ignorant douche bags.

When my father stopped eating dinner with us, Mom brought up his chewing again, saying, "Well, at least there will be no mouth-breathing." Then she said, "I don't know if I love him anymore, Nanette. Does that make you hate me?"

It was a shitty trick to play—her being honest like that—when I was just starting to be honest myself. It didn't seem like everyone could or should be honest at the same time—like maybe the structure of the world wasn't built to handle such mass amounts of truth. Or maybe I sensed the cracks in my parents' marriage long ago, and that's what had finally freed me to start being me no matter the cost.

I had Alex and my secret world with Booker, both of which were so much better than anything my high school or my family had to offer.

"I don't think it really matters, Mom," I said. "Because I won't be here forever, will I?"

My mom looked at me for a moment and then she started to cry.

13

The Boy Can Be a Boy

SO I PLAYED THE CYCLOPS

By Alex Redmer

There's a place where middle
School kids go to fight
And everyone knows where it is
Even the teachers and parents
It's past the playground
On the other side of a hill
Atop which kids can look down
And jeer and snarl and clap
As noses explode and

Knees launch up into groans
And shirts are ripped

I go there now even
Though I am too old
And tall enough to cast
A shadow for miles
And I close one eye
So the kids will think I am
A Cyclops who moans and
Grunts instead of speaking

I go because there is often a
Kid who reminds me of me
When I was in middle school—
Round, red-cheeked, outnumbered
With his fists up just below his glasses
Showing infinitely more guts than
The cocky boy who had the crowd
On his side before he even lifted
His symphony-conductor hands

I usually just yell and moan and play
The monster until everyone runs away
And I'm left with the round lonely boy
Who was me just a few years ago
And I'll tell him middle school

Doesn't
Last
Forever
He doesn't ever believe me
But I can tell he's always glad
I stopped by

This one time I came too late
And the pretty, thin boy
Had the ugly, round
Boy on his back, pinned
Knees on elbows and
Pretty was slapping Ugly
Whose red tear-streaked cheeks
Made the crowd roar
And so I opened both eyes
Became me again
Ran down the hill
Picked up the pretty boy by the
Belt and collar and threw him
High into the air
So that he would know
What it feels like to fall

His head hit the ground first—hard
Enough for grass stains
On his cheek and nose
And I sat on his chest

And I slapped his face
And I told him that his days
Were numbered
And today was zero

I am the Bubblegum Reaper!
I am the Bubblegum Reaper!
I am the Bubblegum Reaper!
I am the Bubblegum Reaper!
I am the Bubblegum Reaper!
I said with each slap
And then I released him like
A fish you catch in polluted
Water and cannot eat

The young round boy stayed behind
When the rest left and he said,
"They're gonna kill me tomorrow"
So I walked that kid home
And I talked to his mom
Who fed me dinner
And I told her she needed
To help
Or at least notice

I went to the old middle school
The next day after high school
And the round kid was looking scared

Again, surrounded by pretty boys
So I played the Cyclops once more
And they all ran, like pretty boys do

I taught the kid to close
One eye and moan
Like a monster
Whenever the pretty boys
Get too close
And now as he waves his arms
Over his head screaming
He is almost
A Cyclops too
But not quite yet
It's okay because pretty boys
They don't know
The
Difference
Most
Of
The
Time
And so
The boy can be a boy
A little bit longer

14

Shifted the Conversation Like a Knife Across My Throat

The soccer team kept winning games without me. Shannon kept running to the flag and crossing the ball, and other girls started to score, and soon the hateful glances I was receiving in the hallway turned into no glances at all. Maybe I was far enough away from the cage. Maybe they couldn't whack me anymore.

Free from varsity-soccer-cult rules, I began sitting on an outdoor bench during lunch periods to read Alex's poetry or *The Bubblegum Reaper*, because we were trying to determine once and for all if Wrigley had fallen for Stella or Lena and were certain that there must be a clue we were missing.

Alex had written a poem called "So I Played the Cyclops," which thrilled and scared me simultaneously. When he gave me a traced copy, he said it was based on an experience he had "not so long ago," when he started hanging around his old middle school, looking for lonely kids who needed help. He did this because he used to fantasize about someone coming to help him when he was being picked on in middle school. He also did it to be like his hero, Wrigley.

The poem made me think about the high school boys who used to come to my middle school with bottles of peach schnapps, looking to bribe younger girls into giving them head. Alex was the opposite of those boys at the center of our middle school sex scandal. I loved him for that. But the rage that was so evident in his poetry was a little frightening, too. I didn't want to date a Cyclops.

"Did you really throw some eighth grader through the air?" I asked him after I had read the poem. We were parked in a field with the Jeep's top down, looking up at a hunter's moon glowing like an enormous flaming pumpkin just over the distant trees. Alex wanted me to listen to a song called "Midnight Surprise" by Lightspeed Champion in the open fall air. It was a really cool song. Weird in a good way. And almost ten minutes long. After it was over, I told him I enjoyed the experience, and we talked about the lyrics at length. Then I said, "Did you really slap the pretty boy in your poem? You must have been twice his size."

"So was Wrigley when he held that kid underwater. The kid who was spinning Unproductive Ted. Remember?"

"Yeah, but that was just a fictional story."

"No, it wasn't. *Wake up, princess*," he said, referencing "Midnight Surprise."

"You think Booker really did that? You think he actually almost drowned a little kid?"

"Sometimes you have to fight against it," Alex said. "If you don't fight against it, you lose yourself."

"Fight against *what*?"

"Everything and everyone who make you feel small, insignificant."

"You can fight with poetry."

"Sometimes words just aren't enough for the situation at hand."

"Yeah, but violence? That's never good."

"Not good, but sometimes *necessary* when people try to make you believe you are secondary or that you shouldn't even exist. Why do you think we study wars in history class? How many months do we spend on World War II alone? When someone evil crosses that line—like Hitler or Mussolini or Tojo or more recently Hussein and bin Laden—it's time to fight. That's what they teach us. So why is it okay for our government to drop bombs on people and kill with guns, but we aren't supposed to use our fists to protect ourselves? This country was founded on and by violence. Our ancestors played the Cyclops when we wanted to steal the land from the indigenous people who were here before us. FDR and Truman both played the Cyclops during World War II. Bush played the Cyclops after 9/11, too."

I'd never heard Alex speak so intensely. I couldn't tell if he was serious or just riffing on ideas, like in his poems, so I said, "Maybe so. But you can't compare middle school kids to Hitler and bin Laden!"

"Both Hitler and bin Laden were once fourteen."

"And you haven't been elected president of the United States of America!"

"Not yet," he said, and then laughed, which made me believe that he was just talking shit—that it was all theoretical.

"You also have to be careful not to make others feel small and insignificant, right?" I said. "You don't want to become what you hate. You can't just go all vigilante. What if everyone did that?"

He was quiet for a time, and then he said, "How did it feel to give your soccer team two middle fingers? To say 'motherfucking' in front of your coach?"

"Truthfully?" I said, and then laughed. *Motherfucking amazing.*

"Maybe you held back for too long and then you had to explode. Maybe there was no middle ground left. Sometimes we need to get violent with our words because no one is listening otherwise."

"Yeah, but I didn't physically hurt anyone."

Alex looked up at the hunter's moon, which had turned from orange to bloodred, and when he didn't say anything in response, I said, "What happened to the kid in the poem? The round one with the glasses? The kid *the pretty boys* wanted to fight?"

"Oliver?"

"His name is Oliver?"

"Yeah. *There's no such thing as fiction.* We actually hang out now." Alex gave me a devilish grin, like he had been leading me to Oliver all along. Like this whole conversation was planned. "You wanna meet him?"

"Seriously?"

"I've kind of been waiting for the right time to introduce you two."

"You have?"

"No time like the present. Let's go."

Alex started the Jeep and turned up his favorite band, Los Campesinos!

"This song's called 'In Medias Res,'" he said. "It's Latin. Know what that means?"

I shook my head.

"'Into the midst.' It's also a storytelling technique. You start in the middle of things. With action. No setup. Just get to the heart of it right away. Like when a war film opens up in the middle of a battle before you even know who's fighting or about what. 'In Medias Res.'"

"And it's how we met. In medias res. At Booker's. Over dinner," I said.

"Yeah, it was, wasn't it?"

I loved talking with Alex about music and writing, mostly because it was so natural—almost like watching a hunter's moon rise, something I had never even thought of doing before Booker introduced me to Alex. And yet it was all so refreshingly odd, too.

I smiled at him, reached over, and squeezed his thigh through his dark jeans, and then he turned up the song even more and pushed down on the gas pedal.

We drove for about twenty minutes or so before he turned down the radio and pulled up to a tiny house with dirty green siding in a poorer neighborhood I didn't know.

"Shhh," Alex said, holding his index finger up to his lips, and then I followed him around to the back of the house. He knocked on the first-floor window three times. The shade went up, and then Oliver's big glasses were looking at us through a screen, which was quickly raised so that we could climb through the window, which we did.

Oliver looked a lot like Ralphie from *A Christmas Story*.

"Is this your woman?" the kid asked Alex, trying to sound manly and tough maybe.

"Um... *what*?" I said.

"I'm sorry," Oliver said from his wooden desk chair, and then looked at his lap.

Alex punched him lightly on the arm and said, "Oliver, this is my good friend, Nanette. Nanette, this is my main man, Oliver. Good people meet good people."

"Alex talks about you all the time," Oliver said, and then pushed his heavy glasses up his nose. "You're even prettier than he makes you out to be."

"Thank you," I said, blushing. No one other than my dad and mom had ever called me pretty before.

"But it's her intelligence that makes me all hot and bothered," Alex said, and then sort of bear-hugged Oliver, who squealed with delight. It was like they were brothers.

The bedroom door opened and a middle-aged woman stuck her head in. "You're allowed to use the front door, Alex. And you're welcome anytime, day or night. You know that."

"The front door just isn't as much fun," Alex said, and then smiled at her.

"This *the one*?" She glanced over at me.

Alex said, "The one and only Nanette O'Hare."

"You're a very lucky girl. This boy is a saint. *A true living saint right here on Earth.*"

"Okay, Mom," Oliver said. "You can leave now."

The woman smiled at her son, and then to me she said, "Well, nice to meet you . . . what's your name again?"

"Nanette."

"French?"

"I'm American."

"Good. I like Americans." She shut the door.

"Can we finally show her now?" Alex asked Oliver.

"I don't know. I just met her, like, ten seconds ago!"

"Come on. Let's show her. Look at her face. She's trustworthy."

Oliver looked at me and asked, "Are you for Lena or Stella?"

"You've read *The Bubblegum Reaper*?" I asked.

"Only a million times."

Alex said, "I got him hooked a little early, maybe."

I looked around Oliver's bedroom and saw pictures of flowers. Endless flowers. They were all cut out of magazines and Scotch-taped to the wall—roses, lilies, daffodils, carnations, hydrangea, and hundreds of others I couldn't even name. In between the flowers were pictures of Oliver's mom and a dozen or so pictures of Alex and Oliver together. There was one of them lying together in a huge field of yellow dandelions. The shot was taken from above—like someone had to climb a tree to get them both in the frame.

Alex pointed to the pic. "We used a timer and some rope to get that. I had to drop from a high branch and lie down before the click.

We tried maybe fifty times before we got what we were after, which is why I'm sweaty in the picture. But don't you think it's cool?"

"Yeah," I said.

"Stella or Lena?" Oliver said, staying focused.

"Lena," I said.

"See, I told you," Alex said. "She's on your team, bro."

"What's with all the flowers?" I asked.

"Boys can like flowers," Oliver said a little defensively.

"I like flowers. I'm a boy," Alex said. "It's absolutely true."

"Wrigley likes flowers, too," Oliver said. "Look."

He pulled out an old yearbook. It was red, and *1967* was printed on the cover in oversize gold numbers.

"What is that?" I asked.

Oliver thumbed through the senior portraits until he got to the *Bs. "Here."* He poked the page with his finger.

Nigel Wrigley Booker

"Nothing is more perfect than a flower." Nigel Wrigley Booker does not describe himself as a loner. He is independent. He has his books and his poetry and his own writing. He didn't particularly enjoy high school and is hoping that life on the other side is a bit kinder and more humane. (Death to gym class!) He hopes to publish a book of poetry at some point in his life but will write poetry regardless of whether anyone wants to read it. Favorite poem: "Fern Hill" by Dylan Thomas. Best friend: Lazy Sam, the turtle on the rock behind the high school.

When I looked at the black-and-white photo, I could see clearly that it was Booker when he was our age—only in the senior photo, he looks older than Alex and me, probably because black-and-white photos make everyone look older. He's also wearing a skinny tie in the shot, and an old-fashioned sports coat. His hair is shaved tight to his skull, making his ears look even more gigantic. He's not smiling, and he looks sort of beaten down.

"Where did you get this?" I asked.

"eBay," Oliver said. "Alex found out where Booker went to high school—only a half hour's drive away from here—and when he graduated, by writing him letters. And then we searched the Internet for months for this baby. A 1967 graduate, Eddie Alva, died, and his son sold absolutely everything he found in his apartment. Lucky for us. We got this for only four dollars plus postage!"

"It gets better," Alex said. "Show her."

Oliver thumbed through more senior pictures until he got to the *T*s.

"Here are the twins," Oliver said. "Sandra Tackett and Louise Tackett."

They look so much alike you would have sworn that someone had printed the same photo twice by accident. Their dark hair is parted down the middle and hangs just past their shoulders; their necks are equally slender; they're both wearing a string of pearls and a dark scoop-neck sweater with a lily pinned just under the right collarbone. It's impossible to tell them apart. They even have the same exact write-up.

"What you see isn't always what you get." The Tackett twins enjoy tricking their fellow students. It is impossible to tell them apart, not only because they dress the same, but also because they speak and act exactly the same as well. They are virtually interchangeable and are rumored to be telepathic, although they deny this claim. Sandra and Louise were both crowned junior prom queen because the student body could not tell them apart on the night of, nor could their prom dates. Favorite song: "Paperback Writer" by the Beatles. Best friend: my twin.

Oliver said, "Look at the left corner of Louise's smile. It's slightly lower than Sandra's by a centimeter or so. Like maybe she's a bit sadder and not really wanting to go along with the joke. Perhaps because she's not who her sister wants her to be? But not strong enough to be her own person. The type of girl who would confess to a turtle when no one else was around!"

"A stretch," Alex said, "because that smile difference is barely perceivable. And even if there *is* a discrepancy between their smiles, maybe it was Sandra who put the song 'Paperback Writer' in the shared bio to let Booker know that she had faith in him even back then. And that's why she's smiling harder. Booker surely told her that he wanted to write a novel when they were talking in the woods. She knew he'd get the reference. It's mind-numbingly obvious after all. Maybe even prophetic, since *The Bubblegum Reaper* was never published in hardback."

"Wait," I said. "So you're saying that you have the Thatch

twins' real names and yet you haven't done anything with them? You haven't done any other research?"

"Oh, *we have*," Oliver said. "But there's a little problem."

"And you're not going to like it," Alex said.

"Why?"

"Your girl Louise is no longer with us."

"Guess what year she died?" Oliver said.

"How would I know that?"

"Nineteen eighty-nine," Alex said.

Oliver said, "One year after—"

"*The Bubblegum Reaper* was published," we all said in unison.

"Which might explain why Booker never resold the rights after he reacquired them," Alex said.

"Why?" I said.

"*Because*," Oliver explained, "he wrote it for Louise Tackett. He was trying to win her heart! So once her heart stopped beating, there was no point for the book to be in print any longer. At least as far as Booker was concerned. It's not a novel but a public love letter to one woman."

"*Unless*," Alex said, "he had the twins mixed up, and I was right all along and Sandra Tackett was his great love—the twin who talked to turtles in the woods. Only Booker had it wrong the whole time, thinking he had that moment in the woods with Louise when it was actually Sandra, which would be the greatest tragedy I've ever heard of. It would even beat *Romeo and Juliet*. Only it would mean Booker's Juliet isn't actually dead but has been waiting all these years for him to figure it out!"

"But then why wouldn't she come forward when she read the book?" I asked.

"Exactly!" Oliver said.

"Maybe she never read the book," Alex said. "I mean, present company excluded, do you personally know anyone else who *has*—besides the teachers who gave it to us? *Anyone?*"

"Good point," I said. "So why not track down Sandra Tackett?"

"Oh, *we have*," Oliver said. "Like everyone else in South Jersey, she lives about twenty minutes from here."

"So what are you waiting for?" I asked.

"It's a gamble," Alex said. "What if I'm wrong? What if Sandra Tackett gets mad when she reads the book? And what if Booker doesn't want us to get involved? I mean—he's forbidden us from even talking about *The Bubblegum Reaper*. What if Booker gets so mad at us that he'll never speak with us again? We could be digging up an ugly skeleton here."

I thought about how I'd lost Mr. Graves in an instant, and I didn't think I could handle losing Booker, too.

"I've voted yes," Oliver said. "Alex voted no. You're the tiebreaker."

"I am?"

"Yeah," Alex said. "We agreed to let you end the stalemate. So your call, Nanette."

"You really have her address?"

"Yep. She's widowed," Oliver said. "And pretty hot for an old lady. So if Alex is right..."

"Sometimes we go to her street and watch her do yard work from a distance," Alex said. "She has a fantastic garden—vegetables and flowers. Her sunflowers grew seven feet before she cut them down this fall! And she's spry for an older woman, moving around on her hands and knees quick as a spider. We've been scouting her for old Booker. It's the least I could do after he wrote me so many letters and encouraged my writing—sending me so many book recommendations. Introducing me to Larkin and Bukowski. He's the best teacher I've ever had, and he isn't even officially my teacher. But I still worry about being wrong. Messing it all up. Crossing a line."

There was that saying again, "crossing a line," and I thought about Mr. Graves once more. Visiting the real live Stella Thatch, meeting another character from *The Bubblegum Reaper*, was almost impossible to resist—just like kissing Mr. Graves on Valentine's Day—so hadn't I learned my lesson? But this was different, because I would be doing it for Booker and not me. Or would I be?

"So what do you vote, Nanette?" Oliver said. "Moment of truth."

"I have to think about it," I said.

"Crushing anticlimax!" Oliver said, and then his mom came in right on cue.

"School night for Oliver," she said, as if Oliver were six years old and not fourteen.

"Mom!" Oliver said.

"We're going," Alex said. "Talk tomorrow, Oliver."

"Nice meeting you, Nanette," Oliver said. "Good to have you on the team."

"Good to be on the team," I said, and then as I waved goodbye I saw the same goodness in Oliver's face that I had seen in Alex's many times. I started to wonder if that was what the bullies were after. Did they want to smash that goodness out of every-one? Alex was always calling the bullies "pretty boys," maybe to emasculate them, maybe because they were the most popular and therefore considered the best-looking—but to me, being pretty wasn't something to be ashamed of, and Oliver and Alex had a soft beauty in their glances and smiles that I found to be radiant. Maybe not in a sexual way, but in a way that makes everything okay, if only for a second or two. Mr. Graves had this quality, too.

Once we were in the Jeep, I said, "You bastard! Sitting on all this info!"

"Couldn't betray my partner's confidence. Guy code."

"So many secrets," I said. "Kind of sexy."

"I am a man of infinite mysteries." He raised his left eyebrow.

"You know that both of your theories are wildly implausible. I'm not sure I really saw a difference in the smiles. 'Paperback Writer' was a very popular song—the favorite of many teenagers back then? *And* there are twins in almost every big high school class. The similarities between the real yearbook names and the ones in *The Bubblegum Reaper* are striking—but maybe Booker took fragments of his high school experience and fictionalized the whole thing?"

"And yet he's always saying, 'There's no such thing as fiction.'"

"True."

"And these details and theories, flimsy or solid or somewhere in between—they're what we have—*all* we have—to go on."

"Why do we have to go on *anything*? Why can't we just let things with Booker be?" I said, even though—deep down—I knew I'd never be able to resist the proposed adventure.

96

"You have to find something to believe in—root for. You know? 'A life lived well gets messy,'" he said, quoting *The Bubblegum Reaper*. "It's maybe—I don't know. It's just what we have right now. The thing we do together. You and me and Oliver, too. I mean, we wouldn't even know each other if it weren't for *The Bubblegum Reaper*. You and I would have never kissed if Booker didn't write the book. And now we can use the same novel that changed our lives for the better to improve the author's life. How amazing is that? It's the literary equivalent of helping and repaying God."

"Assuming that your theory about Stella Thatch is correct, of course. Which is a gamble. If you're wrong, things could get ugly."

"Well, sometimes you have to gamble."

"So why did you vote no?"

"So we'd need a tiebreaker and Oliver would be cool with my cutting you in."

It was flattering, but I flashed on Mr. Graves again and started to feel nervous, so I changed the subject by saying, "Oliver loves you."

"Yeah, well," he said, and then grinned.

"You shared it with him—our novel."

"He needs it just as much as we do. Don't you think?"

I leaned over and kissed Alex full on the lips, and then I said, "Why didn't you have a girlfriend before we met? How did you ever fall to me?"

He smiled, put on the Los Campesinos! song "What Death Leaves Behind," and then shifted into gear.

It was a cool fall night, especially with the top down, so we blasted the heat, which felt nice on my hands and feet, even though it burned just a tiny bit.

When we reached my home, Alex said, "You know we're going to visit Sandra Tackett."

"I know," I said. "But I'm not so sure we should."

"I think we have to."

"Why exactly is that again?"

"Because if we don't try, we'll never know."

"Know what?"

"That love can win."

"Can love win?" I said, but not sarcastically. My voice sort of quivered a bit, and I realized that my heart was pounding and it felt like someone was pressing a finger into the spot where my throat meets my chest. We were messing around with dangerous forces, and Alex was only slightly less afraid than I was.

Under the streetlight in front of my home, we kissed for a time right in full view of the neighbors, but I didn't even care.

I grabbed his hand and put it on my chest, and he didn't pull away.

He was gentle, and it was nice to be touched.

When we finished making out, I said, "You know what? I didn't see any signatures in Eddie Alva's yearbook."

"That's because there weren't any."

"Not even one? *Nobody* signed it?"

"Nope."

"So why do you think he kept it all these years? If he didn't have any friends in high school? It's so sad."

"I don't know."

"What does his senior bio say?"

"There isn't one. Just his picture and name: Eddie Alva. He looks tortured in the photo. No smile. Definitely not one of the pretty boys. Heavy eyebrows. Crooked nose. Just by looking into his eyes, you can tell he hated high school. I think the blank space under him says everything. Maybe the metaphorical equivalent of your double middle finger to the soccer team."

"And yet he kept his yearbook?"

"Maybe he did it for us, Nanette."

It was tempting to believe that—there was poetry in such thinking. Like maybe the universe was conspiring in our favor all of a sudden. But it felt a little fucked, too. Eddie Alva didn't even know we existed when he died. And his keeping a yearbook for almost five decades, a yearbook that no one signed, was depressing enough to make you want to curl up in your room alone and weep for him. He reproduced, so maybe he had known love for a little while, I told myself. He had sex at least once with someone. There was that. And maybe he loved his high school classmates in a strange sort of way—the way you sometimes love the villains in your favorite stories just because they are an integral part of the plot. Maybe it was what he had, Eddie Alva, this set of classmates to populate that part of his personal history. And I thought about how I sort of missed Shannon in a weird, sad way, even though I definitely didn't want to hang out with her anymore. I'd probably be thinking about Shannon and all my soccer teammates until I died. The Rainbow Dragons were a part of my psyche for good, bad, or indifferent, and that was just the way it was. And then it hit me: None of them would probably be signing my yearbook, either, because they no longer would even make eye contact with me, which was certainly sad, but I was also okay with it somehow.

When I finally went inside, Mom was sitting on the living room couch. "Nice show out there."

The funny thing is—I think she was proud of me. I was growing up, finally making out with a boy, doing age-appropriate things. What she did when she was my age, back when she was a cheerleader. But then Mom shifted the conversation like a knife across my throat.

"In other news," she said, "your father moved out."

"*What?*"

"Yep."

"When?"

"About three hours ago. You missed his big blowup."

"He's already gone?"

"You can call him on his cell if you want an explanation."

"What's *your* explanation?"

"It doesn't have anything to do with you."

"Is it because I quit soccer?"

"Don't be ridiculous. Of course not," Mom said, looking out the window, avoiding eye contact.

"When is he coming back?"

"I really don't think he is, sweetie. I'm so sorry."

There were tears in her eyes, but I could tell that she felt it was all for the best—that this was a long time in the making, and perhaps final.

From my bedroom, I called my father. When he answered, I could hear a news broadcast playing in the background—and he echoed my mother, saying their breakup had nothing to do with my quitting soccer or me at all. "I think we both knew we'd part ways after you left for college. But we just couldn't make it that long. We were close, but we couldn't do it. I'm sorry. People fall out of love, Nanette. It's just the way it is. But we both love you the same as we ever did. That will never change."

So everyone was sorry.

As if that helped.

Dad said we'd go out to dinner twice a week and then we'd see how things went while he found a more permanent place to stay, as he was currently in a motel. I would live with Mom in the house where we had all lived for my entire life.

I asked if either of them was seeing anyone else, and they said they weren't. They each just wanted to be alone for a time. They preferred nobody to each other, which made it all that much worse.

Right then and there, I mentally shifted my allegiance and began rooting very hard for team Stella Thatch and Sandra Tackett.

There was that possibility, at least.

I wanted to believe that love could win in the end.

I called Alex from my bedroom and said, "I vote yes."

15

This Broken-Family Club

"My parents separated. My dad moved out a few days ago," I said to Booker as we sat in his sunroom. "It's kind of funny. Just as soon as I fall in love for the first time, Mom and Dad call it quits—like they were waiting for me to take over for them. Carry high the love banner because their arms were too tired."

"Well, at least you and Alex are getting along famously."

"How did you know that Alex and I would be a match?"

"Oh, I just had a hunch."

"But the timing. I mean—it was like you knew I'd need a boyfriend when my parents broke up. You had a feeling that all this was necessary. *You knew.* But how?"

"I definitely did *not* know anything about your parents' situation. Let's not entertain magical thoughts. It's just that all eighteen-year-olds need to be in love. It's why we have things like proms, even though proms are not for everyone. You're at a time in your life when you need to feel and believe wildly—that's just the way it is."

"Were you ever in love, Booker?"

"Sure."

"What happened?"

"Nothing, unfortunately."

"Why?"

"Lack of courage, mostly."

I thought about Wrigley, who turns and runs just as he's about to ring his prom date's doorbell. And how the real-life twins were the prom queens. Had Booker been at the real-life prom? Or maybe had he put on a tuxedo and held a finger up to a doorbell only to flee at the last possible moment? "Do you wish you had done things differently?"

"Of course. Pretty much everyone does."

"What was her name?"

"Why do you assume it was a her?"

"Was it a him?"

"No, it was a her."

I laughed. "Tell me about this special mystery woman."

He looked away.

"Did you never tell her how you felt? Like Wrigley in—"

"Stop right there," Booker said, and then pointed a finger at my face. "We shall not be discussing my failed novel."

"It definitely was *not* a failure."

"By what standard did it succeed?"

"It's my favorite novel. Alex's, too. And this kid Oliver who Alex—"

"I know all about Oliver. Alex writes about him constantly. But is that the purpose of writing a novel—to be someone's favorite novelist? Is that why we write or make art? Do you think that's why I wrote that book? For you? You and Alex and Oliver didn't even exist when I went mad for literature and sent that collection of desperate words to New York City. I didn't write it for you. No, I certainly did not." There was anger in his voice, which was not like Booker.

"For whom did you write it, then?" I asked.

He smiled and said, "You won't get your answers that easily."

I nodded, and then I had a random thought. "You never talk about your parents. Do you have a good relationship with them?"

"I didn't know Mom. She left my father when I was little. For a better-looking and wealthier man she'd met while working as a waitress. Dr. Farrell. I believe they had a torrid affair in the back alley and then the local hotel and finally in the man's mansion across town from where I lived. On the other side of the tracks, as they say."

"So she left you and your father?"

"Yes, she did. I guess I can't blame her. It wasn't really a happy home. I like to think at least *she* was happy. My father was a weak man. I never really saw her after she moved out."

"She just left you behind?"

"Completely forgot about me. Had new children."

"And that's why you don't trust women?"

"Are you Sigmund Freud now? Should I lie down on this couch?"

"I'm sorry."

"I trust you."

"You don't trust me enough to tell me about your great love," I said, and suddenly I was full of electricity again—like I was close enough to just go for it. "Was she by any chance a twin?"

Booker didn't speak for a second, which was unusual. A sadness darkened his face before he caught himself and said, "I don't want to talk about my past. How many times have I told you this?"

"Okay," I said. My heart was beating too fast, so I switched gears. "I hate my parents. I love them, too. But mostly, I'm just tired of being around them. Does that make any sense? Loving and hating people at the same time?"

"Yes, I'm afraid it does."

"So what should I be doing now?"

"What do you mean?"

"I don't know. I'm just eighteen, and I know I'm supposed to be going gaga for my last year of high school and applying to colleges and making plans for the rest of my life—but I really don't want to do anything except hang out with Alex and you."

"Well, then be glad we both want to hang out with you, too. What a lucky thing—to have exactly what you want."

"But it can't last. After this year, everything will be different."

"And yet there is now. It's all yours and mine and Alex's. Isn't that divine?"

I smiled and then said, "I went out to dinner with my father last night, and he told me I had to write a fantastic college essay now that I wasn't going to play soccer anymore. He went on and on about it and didn't ask one question about my now. I don't think he even knows about you or Alex."

"His loss," Booker said.

"I wish you were my father."

"Don't wish for stupid things."

"Is it so stupid?"

"If I were your father, we couldn't be friends, now, could we? You would hate me instead of your actual father. And I would feel obligated to make sure you were writing *a fantastic college essay*. We probably wouldn't talk about anything else. And I certainly wouldn't be playing your personal cupid if I were your father. So as you can plainly see, my being your father would ruin absolutely everything."

I thought about it and laughed because it all made so much sense.

"Booker? If she walked into your life again—the love of your life—and she wanted to be with you, would you give love another chance?"

"That's not going to happen."

"But if it could? Theoretically?"

"We're different people now. Pablo Neruda said it better than I can. 'Tonight I Can Write.' Read that poem if you haven't already. You'll fall in love with Neruda and wish you were eighteen when he was—that you knew him in Chile a long time ago. I'd recite it for you now, but it would make me cry, and I hate crying in front of lovely young women."

I swallowed hard and said, " 'There were moments when my love for her made me believe that I was better than I really was— or was it that she made me aware of my own potential, that she made it possible for me to transcend myself and truly become?' Nigel Wrigley Booker, *The Bubblegum Reaper*."

His eyes widened and then he roared, "How did you discover my middle name?"

"I . . ." But I couldn't think up a good explanation on the spot.

"Did Alex tell you that? Did he show you my yearbook?"

I didn't know what to say, so I said nothing. I'd never before seen Booker turn bright red.

"I'm not interested in Sandra Tackett or Louise Tackett, God rest her soul. And I need you to leave now. Right now!"

"I'm sorry," I said. "I was only trying to—"

"Leave me!"

Booker had never yelled at me like that before, either. His face was now turning purple, like he was about to have a stroke or something, and the look in his eyes was devastating, because I saw hatred swirling around his pupils. It scared me, so I left.

On the pavement, I called Alex and tried to tell him everything.

"Sit tight," he said. "I'll be right there."

When he pulled up, Oliver was in the front seat looking glum. His glasses were taped together where the lenses met at the top of his nose, and his cheek was swollen.

"What happened to you?" I asked.

"I could ask you the same," Oliver said.

"Get in," Alex said, and so I did.

We drove to the field where Alex and I had watched the hunter's moon rise, and then we all exchanged information.

The pretty boys had started in on Oliver during lunch period, throwing Tater Tots dipped in ketchup at him, which explained the red spots on his shirt, so he reported them to the lunch monitor, who took two or three of the pretty boys to the principal's office. The rest jumped him on his way home from school, breaking his glasses and leaving bruises on his ribs as punishment for being a "snitch."

"It's like our middle school is a prison and I might get shanked at any second," Oliver said, maybe going for humor, but we didn't laugh.

"I'm going to their houses tonight. I'm going to speak with their fathers," Alex said.

"Don't do that. It will only make things worse for me," Oliver said. Then to me, he said, "So what happened at Booker's place?"

I told them everything, and I got the sense they weren't pleased that I'd leaked information.

"He already knew you had the yearbook," I said in self-defense. "Alex told him."

"You told Booker about the yearbook?" Oliver asked Alex.

"In a roundabout way. Just testing the waters, so to speak."

"But we didn't vote on it," Oliver said. "We vote on everything!"

"True. My bad," Alex said.

"*My bad?*" Oliver said.

I was sensing some tension, so I got to the point. "I voted yes to making contact with Sandra Tackett. Let's go right now."

"*Really?*" Oliver said, which let me know Alex hadn't told him yet.

"Yes. I'm in. One hundred percent."

"Well, all right, then," Alex said. "You heard the lady."

"But my shirt is full of ketchup stains," Oliver protested. "I don't want to meet the real live Stella Thatch like this!"

"We'll swing by your house first so you can grab the yearbook, the extra photocopy of *The Bubblegum Reaper* you made, and a clean shirt," Alex said.

"I also need to shower. You don't meet a Sandra Tackett every day," Oliver said, and then we were off.

As we were driving, Alex kept looking at me in the rearview mirror, since I was sitting in the back. Whenever he caught my eye, he would smile brightly, as if we were in on a private joke—or maybe it was like Oliver was our kid and we were planning some sort of surprise birthday party for him, as weird as that sounds. But I got the sense that we weren't just doing this for ourselves but because Oliver had had a terrible day at school, too. We were trying to right that wrong. It was a relief that Alex didn't seem mad at me for upsetting Booker, because when I'd left Booker's house, it felt a lot like when I had tried to kiss Mr. Graves.

While Oliver showered and changed, I slid up into the Jeep's front passenger seat.

"Booker totally freaked out when I brought up the Tackett twins," I said. "I'm sorry. I shouldn't have done it. But you already wrote him about the yearbook, so you can't be too mad at me."

"Yeah, I'm not," he said, and then laughed.

There was a devilish twinkle in his eye.

"You know more than you're letting on," I said.

"Maybe."

"What game are you playing?"

"No game."

"You know, I asked Booker why he never talks about his mother and he told me about—"

"How she had an affair with a doctor and left him behind. It's sad."

"You knew?"

"Yeah."

"Well, it made me realize that you never talk about your mother, either."

He shrugged. "She left me and my father, too. Only there was no rich doctor or a mansion or any wild affair. She just left us when I was seven. It crushed my father, who sort of became a zombie afterward. He's a nice guy who bought me this kick-ass Jeep, but he's not really present most of the time. Not like Booker has been, anyway. Mom sends me a Christmas card every year with a hundred-dollar bill in it. But my dad has enough bucks to make that seem sort of sad and irrelevant. I don't spend those hundred-dollar bills. I give them to the first person I come across who looks depressed. Always a total stranger. I fold the bill up so that I can palm it, then I reach out and shake a miserable person's hand, transferring the money—but I never, ever talk to the person. If I let them thank me, it would ruin everything, so I just walk away quickly. That's been a Christmas tradition for some time now. Other than that, I don't really hear from my mom at all."

"Do you not trust women now?"

"What?" he said, and then laughed.

I let it go and then said, "What about Oliver's dad?"

"Pretty much the same story as ours."

"Ours?"

"Your dad just left, too."

It shocked me at first when he said that, but then I realized I was indeed part of this broken-family club now. Even still, I said, "He didn't exactly leave me. We have dinner a few times a week."

"Does that make you feel any better?"

I looked away.

Oliver bounded out his front door wearing a pair of backup glasses too small for his face and a new button-down shirt. He had the yearbook and the photocopied *Bubblegum Reaper* in his arms. "You stole my seat!"

"You forgot to call shotgun. Get in the back, my man," Alex said, and then we were on our way to Sandra Tackett's house.

16

Using the Same Basement You Were Currently Locked Away In

At a white ranch home with two apple trees in front of it and a large flower garden to its right, a woman about Booker's age answered the door and said, "Can I help you?"

She was wearing an orange cotton dress with a white sweater. Her hair was gray but stylish, with a little wave on the right side of her face. She had on pewter eye shadow, which I immediately wanted to wear myself, even though I had never before worn eye shadow. Hers didn't make her look slutty like most of my classmates—who wore eye shadow heavy as porn stars—but mysterious and maybe even regal, like a queen.

"Are you Sandra Tackett?" Alex said.

"That's me. Now, who are you three?"

Alex introduced us all.

"Is this you?" Oliver said, and held up the 1967 yearbook opened to her photo.

"Where on earth did you get that?" she said, and then laughed in this very good way. "I'm actually the one next door. My twin sister and I thought it would be funny if we tricked everyone. She was photographed as me and vice versa."

Alex and Oliver and I exchanged glances.

"Now—what, may I ask, brought you to my front door wielding a yearbook?"

I said, "We're friends of Nigel Booker. Do you remember him? He was in your class."

"How do you know Nigel?" she asked.

"We're technically his fans," Alex said.

"Nigel has fans now?"

"Have you read his novel?" Oliver asked.

"I have not," she said.

"It was published in 1988, but it went out of print shortly after," Alex said. "We think that two of the characters might be based on you and your sister."

"Well, I'll be," she said, and then put her hand on her chest as if to suggest she was highly flattered. "Why would he write about *us*?"

Her asking that question seemed bad for Team Stella. If Sandra had been the real-life twin in the woods with Wrigley, she would know exactly why he would write about them. But then again, that was almost fifty years ago, so maybe she had forgotten. She also could have just been playing dumb, like she did for her twin—well, in the novel at least.

Regardless of whose theory was right, I could tell that the woman in front of us was excited, which scared me, because what if she was the bad twin in the novel? There was no way she would enjoy the read if we had it wrong. It seemed like we were playing with emotional dynamite.

"And it's a love story," Oliver said. "Maybe even *a love letter*."

"A mystery we're hoping you can solve," Alex said. "We'd like to interview you after you read the book."

"Why don't you ask Nigel whatever questions you have? He's the author. So certainly he can fill in the blanks."

"He won't talk about the novel anymore," Alex said. "He's put a moratorium on book discussions."

"Why?"

"Well," Alex said, "we believe he's heartbroken. And that it might be you he's pining for."

"That sounds positively salacious!" the woman said with a huge smile on her face and both hands over her heart now, which seemed like a good sign for Team Stella. "Where can I get a copy of this novel?"

"It's out of print, like we said," Oliver said. "But we made you a photocopy."

Alex held up the photocopied manuscript. "Again, we're hoping you'll be willing to read it and then answer a few questions for us."

"Well, it certainly sounds interesting. And I have nothing but time these days."

Alex gave her the manuscript, we agreed to return at the end of the week, and then there was no turning back.

"Shotgun!" Oliver yelled, relegating me to the backseat.

Alex and I went inside to speak with Oliver's mother when we dropped him off. Oliver marched straight back to his room and pulled the door shut a little harder than necessary. Alex said he would visit the fathers of the boys who had broken Oliver's glasses, but she needed to talk to his school. She agreed, but I got the feeling that she wasn't going to follow through, because she kept saying, "I'll call in a few days—once everything calms down," even though Alex kept saying it was important to call right away.

"He needs an advocate. Two would be even better," Alex said, and I could tell that he was really trying to do the right thing, to make a difference in Oliver's life, but at the same time I wanted to remind him that he, too, was just a kid and not Oliver's father.

Oliver was in his room, but the house was so small that he had to have heard the whole conversation. At one point, I got up and checked on him. He was pretending to read *The Bubblegum Reaper*, although he glanced over at me real quick when I knocked and opened the door.

"You okay?" I asked.

"Yeah. *You* okay?"

"Yeah."

I didn't know what else to say, so I went back into the living room and waited for Alex to finish. He phoned Oliver's school, and when the answering machine came on, he held out the phone to Oliver's mom, but she wouldn't take it. Alex left a message asking the school to call her as soon as possible.

When Alex parked his Jeep in front of my home, he said, "You didn't really say anything to Sandra Tackett when we visited her today. Oliver and I did all the talking."

"I don't think you should go visiting the fathers of those boys tonight," I said, totally changing the subject.

"Why?"

"Because you're not Oliver's dad. Because you're still a teenager like me. And we have eight months of high school left and—"

"The kid's getting killed every day. We have to do something."

"Kids get killed in every middle school in America."

"Exactly."

"But I feel like I'm getting killed, too, Alex." The words were out of my mouth before I really had a chance to think about what I was saying. "I don't even know what's happening to me anymore."

"What do you mean?"

"So many things are going on all at once, and I just sort of feel unmoored or something."

"Unmoored? Because your dad left?"

"That's part of it."

"And?"

"I'm worried that we just lost Booker, too."

"We didn't. Trust me," Alex said, and then he kissed me on the lips.

He tasted warm and a little sweet from the gum he was chewing.

"Is that Wrigley's Doublemint?" I said, because he was always trying to emulate his favorite fictional character.

"Of course!" he said. "What else would it be?"

For some reason, I got a bad feeling. Chewing that brand of gum was no big deal in and of itself, but I had begun worrying that Alex was taking his hero worship of Wrigley a bit too far.

"What are you going to say to those kids' dads?"

"I'm going to play the Cyclops."

"By doing what, exactly? Waving your hands over your head with one eye closed?"

I didn't mean it to sound sarcastic, but it definitely did.

"You don't know what it's like to be Oliver. Someone has to do something. I'll talk to those fathers. Try to reason with them."

"When I was Oliver's age, everyone used to cough into their hands and say 'dyke' really fast when I walked by. I pretended that it didn't bother me, but it did. I don't know if that's worse than having your glasses broken or not, but kids call me even worse homophobic slurs today."

"Really? Why?"

"I have no idea, since I'm not a lesbian. I don't know why being called a lesbian is such a bad thing anyway. And since I'm not homophobic, why does it even bother me? I can't figure it out."

"What are the names of the boys who do this?"

"Girls do it, too."

"Give me all the names."

"Seriously?"

"Dead serious."

"There are dozens. What would you do if I gave you a list?"

"I'd take care of it."

"What does that mean? You can't fight everyone, Alex."

"Sure you can!" he said, and his voice cracked a little. "You fight everyone who needs fighting or nothing changes! *Nothing!*"

We were silent for a time, and then I said, "Don't get into any trouble tonight. Promise me."

"What sort of trouble do you think I could get into by having a conversation with a bunch of suburban dads?" He smiled at me in a way that let me know the anger had subsided and he had control of himself again. "Will they make me mow their perfectly manicured lawns? Wash their minivans? Have a catch with them?"

"I don't know. I just have a bad feeling, that's all."

"Well, then let's give you that good feeling," he said as he leaned in to kiss me.

We made out for a little and then I said I had to go.

When I went inside, my mother was drinking a bottle of wine alone in the kitchen. Two-thirds already was gone. "You okay, Mom?"

"Yes, I am," she said, slurring her words just a bit, but not too bad. "I was saving this 2002 Diamond Creek Gravelly Meadow for a special occasion, and then I thought tonight could be special if I opened it. Do you think we should update the kitchen? I've been sitting here looking at the appliances, and I feel like they say we're living seven years in the past. We need to catch up!"

"Okay?"

"So update immediately, correct?"

"Like—right now?"

"No time to be in the present *like the present*."

"Can we just keep things the way they are until I graduate? I'm not sure I can handle any more change."

"So wait until summer?"

"Yeah, if possible. I'd appreciate it. There will probably be newer updates by then anyway. Better appliances. Maybe they will have robots that cook the food for you and then clean everything up. Could we wait for those?"

"For you, Nanette," she said, pointing a finger at my face, "I will do this. For you."

"Thanks, Mom."

"Are you using protection with that boy?"

"What?"

"Do you need to be on the Pill?"

"Um, I'm going to my room now."

"Be smart, Nanette. We'll talk more in the morning over breakfast. No unprotected sex! No glove, no love, we used to say!"

I shook my head in disbelief, went up to my room, and lay down on my bed. So many thoughts were swirling around in my mind—I started to feel like I might vomit from dizziness.

I picked up Mr. Graves's copy of *The Bubblegum Reaper*, randomly opened up to page seventy-one, and read these words: "I knew that I had reached the end of childhood once I realized that the adults in my life didn't know any more than I did—and then in a flash I knew that everything that had preceded that exact moment was a sort of game played by the so-called adults who winked at each other when you weren't looking…people who pretended to be things they were not, like Santa Claus, the Easter

Bunny, athletic coaches, teachers, our heroes, too. But the sad truth was that they were no better than we were, and more often than not, they were much worse because they had been here on this planet longer than we had and therefore were able to collect more vices, worries, and sadness."

The words stopped the spinning feeling in my head, if only because it felt as though someone had had all my thoughts before, which was comforting, like knowing that people had survived a tornado using the same basement you were currently locked away in, so I read on until there were no more words left in the book—just as I had so many times before—and only then could I fall asleep.

17

They Didn't Run Away to Save Themselves but Sprinted Right into My Lava

I called Alex's cell phone first thing the next morning, and when he didn't answer, my stomach began to churn. As I walked to school, I kept calling and texting, saying it was important and he should please call as soon as he could. No response. When I checked my cell phone during study hall, there was a voice message from Oliver's mom.

> Alex was arrested last night. He punched the father of
> one of the kids who was picking on Oliver. Police came
> to interview Oliver this morning. I've kept him out of
> school. He's home alone because I have to work. Oliver

is scared. Can you come over to be with him? Alex's father told the police to keep him locked up so that he would learn a lesson. I'm not sure what's going to happen. If you can help get Oliver through the day, I'd really appreciate it. Even if you just check up on him after school. Thank you.

I walked right out of the building, cutting school for just the second time in my life. When I arrived home, I pulled my old ten-speed out of the garage and started pedaling furiously. It took me just over an hour to get to Oliver's home. I locked my bike to the chain-link fence in his backyard and then knocked on his bedroom window three times, like Alex does.

The shade went up, and I could tell by the look on Oliver's face he was disappointed that I wasn't Alex. He opened the screen anyway, and I climbed in.

"You okay?" I asked Oliver.

He nodded, but he didn't look even close to okay.

His hair hadn't been combed, and he was still in his one-piece pajamas, which were spotted with pink roses, so probably intended for girls. I wondered how his mother even found a size that big. And why in the world Oliver would wear them—especially when his mother wasn't around and he was free to do whatever he wanted. The only answer was that he must actually *like* them.

"What happened?" I asked.

"I didn't want Alex to go to their houses. He made me tell him where they lived. He said it would be okay. But now he's in jail."

"What did they say he did?"

"He hit Pete Mandrake's dad. Punched him in the face."

"Why?"

"He doesn't like the pretty boys, or the terrorizers, as he says. I don't like them, either, but this isn't good. He shouldn't have done that."

"Is he still in jail?"

"I think so."

Jail.

It sounded so horrible.

Like a place for other people, but not the ones you know.

"They're going to kill me when I return to school," Oliver said, which was when I noticed the tears forming in the corners of his eyes, so I hugged him and we cried it out. I found myself smoothing his hair, as if I were his mother, which shocked me. I had never thought of myself as maternal before. And yet here I was, comforting this kid.

"This has gotten way too big. Those kids aren't going to touch you now. Everyone will be watching them—their teachers, the police. You'll see. They're going to leave you alone now."

"But what about Alex?"

"How far away is the police station in this town?"

"It's only maybe a twenty-minute walk."

"Do you have a bike?"

"Yeah."

"Okay. Put on your broken glasses. We're going to the police station to see Alex. They might let us in if they feel sorry for you."

It only took us ten minutes to ride our bikes to the police

station, but the woman behind the glass there said we weren't allowed to see Alex. "Can't do it."

I argued with her and showed her Oliver's broken glasses, but she kept shaking her head.

Just when I was about to quit, a police officer behind her looked up and walked over toward us.

"That's the officer who interviewed me today," Oliver said as he waved.

To the woman, the officer said, "Let them in, Cheryl."

She rolled her eyes. "Why have rules if you're just going to break them all the time?"

"Lunch is on me today, okay?"

"If you say so."

Then we heard a buzz, the door opened, and I was introduced to Officer Damon, who had long, skinny sideburns and a small black ribbon tied around his left thumb. We were taken to a back room that looked like the type of place where they interrogate criminals on TV. The walls, ceiling, and floors—everything was concrete except for a wooden table and four chairs. No windows. A bright light hung down from the darkness above. The odd thing was that there was also a small refrigerator in the corner.

"Is this where you try to break criminals?" I asked. "Play good cop and bad cop?"

"No," the officer said. "This is our break room, but not like *break* break. It's where we eat lunch. We don't break anyone down mentally here. We only break bread."

He gave us a big, honest smile.

Despite all that was going on, I smiled back. I liked this cop.

"You're Alex's girlfriend?" he asked.

"We don't use labels, but for all intents and purposes, yes, just to make this go easier. Can we see him?"

"He asked for his 'one phone call,' saying he wanted to contact you, but since he's a minor, we had to contact his parents, and his dad is calling the shots now. But I passed on your cell phone number to Oliver here and his mom. Alex asked me to do that."

"Alex was only trying to make the bullies stop hitting me and breaking my glasses. You don't put people in jail for that," Oliver said. "Like I said this morning. Let him out, please!"

"No, we don't put someone in jail for standing up to bullies," said Officer Damon. "But we do put people in jail for assault and harassment. I'm afraid your friend is in some serious trouble. I'll let you speak. So try to talk some sense into him. We want what's best for everyone. I'm starting to think that he's proud of being in jail. That won't play well when he faces a judge."

"*A judge?*" I asked.

"He assaulted Mr. Peter Mandrake. He's already confessed to the crime. And Mr. Mandrake is pressing charges. It's very real."

I felt my stomach drop again.

"So try to help Alex see the seriousness of it all."

The police officer led us to a small sand-colored jail cell—maybe eight feet by five. There were no windows and the ceiling lights were outside the cell, so shade striped Alex's face. It was horrible to see him locked up like an animal. And yet I was pretty sure he'd acted like an animal that needed to be caged, which scared me.

"Are you okay?" I asked.

"Never been better," Alex said as he hopped off the small bed. "I'm like Henry David Thoreau in here. Nelson Mandela. Jesus Christ, even."

"This isn't a joke. They're pressing charges," I said.

"Let them."

"What?"

"I said let them."

"You could go to jail."

"Already here."

"But for good."

"I doubt it. I'm a minor, first of all. And if they put in jail everyone who ever punched someone, there would hardly be anyone left outside. Why don't they put the kids who punched Oliver in jail? Why isn't anyone asking that?"

"I didn't want you to do this," Oliver said.

"I know," Alex said. "But I had to. And I've never felt more alive in my life. Like I'm finally calling the shots—like they know I won't put up with it anymore."

"Put up with what?" I asked.

He smiled and quoted Wrigley from *The Bubblegum Reaper*: "'They can't make me into a joiner without my permission.'"

I didn't know how to respond. I had underlined that bit many times because I loved it so much, but when it led to seeing the only boy you ever kissed being locked behind bars, the quote took on a different connotation. And I wondered if that was the problem with literature—it made sense only in theoretical situations and didn't often help in real life, where it took a hell of a lot more courage to live than to turn pages all alone, hidden away from the world in a corner or a bed or under a tree.

"I've been writing poetry in here. This experience has been like a muse," Alex said. "Words are bursting out of me. I wrote one about last night called 'There Is Power in Knowing.'"

I noticed the notebook on the bed. A pen was resting on top. I was surprised they let him have these things in a cell.

When he saw me looking, he picked up the notebook, ripped out the poem, folded it up, and handed it to me through the bars.

Worried the cop would confiscate Alex's words, I quickly slid the poem into the front pocket of my jeans. "You can't write poetry in jail, Alex. *Have you lost your mind?*"

"What are you talking about? Jail is the perfect place to write poetry! Poetry is the language of the oppressed!"

He sounded insane.

"But what about our mission?" Oliver said. "What about Sandra Tackett and figuring out the mystery of *The Bubblegum Reaper?*"

"All in good time, my friend. All in good time."

"Alex," I said. "You're in jail. *Jail!* This is serious. You can't just go around punching people in the face."

"I didn't 'just go around punching people in the face.' I was defending Oliver and the rights of all who have ever been in Oliver's position. A principle is at stake here. I'm not afraid to pay the price for my convictions. Wrigley would agree."

"Did you ask Booker what he thought of your ending up in jail?" I asked.

"Booker is an old man. You can't ask an old man to advise you on something that a young man needs to do. But you can read *The Bubblegum Reaper*. You can sure do that. And I've read it a million times!"

A mania had taken up residence in Alex's eyes. It frightened me, but at the same time, it was attractive—the honesty he brought to the conversation. Not even jail could make him put on a mask and lie for everyone else. It was madness, plain and simple, but an alluring sort. It was like standing next to a great fire that dances and warms and illuminates everything—but it also threatens to consume you in the process. How much more of this could I take?

Finally, Officer Damon came back and said we had to leave.

Alex gripped the bars of the prison cell and in a calm voice simply stated, "I love you, Nanette."

A boy had never before proclaimed his love for me like that, and I froze.

We were in a jail.

Oliver and the police officer were there.

But mostly, I wasn't sure whether I loved Alex anymore, and I didn't want to lie, so I just nodded and followed the officer out of the police station.

"Why do you have a black ribbon on your thumb?" Oliver asked the officer when he raised his left hand to buzz us out.

"You don't have to answer that," I said to the officer.

"No," he said. "It's okay. I tie it there so people will ask me that exact question. My son was abducted and killed ten years ago. He was six years old. *Hence the sixth.*" One at a time, Officer

Damon wiggled the fingers and thumb of his right hand. Then he held up the sixth digit—his left thumb. "Six. Would've been about your age now, Nanette. Joshua was walking home from school. He was snatched right in broad daylight. Pulled into a van and then driven away. Just like that—my son was gone. I can't bring Joshua back to life, but I can be a police officer, trying to keep the neighborhood safe. I went into law enforcement because of that incident."

"So you didn't beat up the abductor?" Oliver said. "That's the moral of the story? You did the opposite of what Alex did."

"I wanted to *kill* my son's abductor. He's in jail now. For life. But no, I didn't beat him up. I try to protect others and help kids like your friend Alex back there. People pay a heavy cost for bad decisions. Oftentimes, it's strangers you hurt most."

"I'm sorry your son was taken from you," I said.

Officer Damon nodded and said, "Your friend Alex. He made a bad decision. He doesn't have to make a string of them."

Oliver and I both nodded and left.

I saw the kid home and told him again that the bullies wouldn't be after him now that things had gotten too public, and even though Alex's plan was foolish, it probably would work out the way he wanted it to—meaning Oliver would stop being bullied. "Everyone's paying attention now," I said.

When I had him back in his bedroom, Oliver looked through his window and said, "If Alex gets locked up for a long time—"

"He's not going to—"

"But if he does, will you help me solve the mystery?"

"What mystery?"

"*The Bubblegum Reaper*. The Thatch twins. Sandra Tackett."

"Yeah, I will," I said.

"Promise?"

"Promise."

• • •

In spite of our last sour meeting, I pedaled my bike to Booker's and was relieved when he seemed happy to see me.

"My god, Nanette, why are you shaking like that? Are you okay?"

"I'm sorry to bother you, but something awful has happened."

"Come inside. Tell me everything."

We sat down in his living room, and the words poured out of me. Booker grew more and more tense—like a catapult being tightened before it slingshots its load at an enemy.

When I finished, Booker shook his head. "So he's using my novel as an excuse to go all vigilante on the world. Doesn't he see that I'm a peaceful man now? Why doesn't he emulate *me* instead of my literary character? That's why I pulled the book off the shelves in the first place. Everyone started to go crazy after they read it!"

It was a rare moment of honesty from Booker about *The Bubblegum Reaper*, so I decided to push the issue. "It wasn't because Louise Tackett died? Your refusing to reprint *The Bubblegum Reaper*?"

"Of course not! I can't believe Alex is in jail. How could this have gone so horribly wrong again? It's like I'm cursed!"

"What do you mean, 'again'?" I said.

"Oh, there have been others."

"Others?"

"Young men who have done stupid things after reading my novel. I really thought Alex was smarter than that. That he understood. I've been so selective lately. Do you know how many people contact me about my book? I only interact with the peace-loving ones now. And you—you of all people should have understood and prevented this."

I thought about Alex's violent poetry—wondered how much Booker had read, or had Alex only shown Booker what the old man wanted to read? Then I said, "Understood what?"

"That I help young people with words! Words can help, and kindness and letters and dinners and games of Scrabble and love and talking with others who feel the way you do and sitting in the garden with Don Quixote. We can all learn a great deal from turtles! The book makes you feel. You have to figure out the feelings for yourself. You ponder. Discuss. Reread. And if you do it right, you have a catharsis. That's supposed to make you feel better. It's a soul-cleansing! Purification. That's what *catharsis* means in Greek. Don't they teach you anything in high school these days? What's Oliver going to do if Alex ends up in jail? Does he really think the kid would be better off? Oliver would choose spending quality time with Alex even if it meant being bullied. How obtuse can a young person be? I'm not taking the blame for this one. I never encouraged violence. No one would blame Shakespeare if kids started drinking hemlock and killing each other with broadswords. Why do I even try with you young people? I think I may be done with teenagers altogether. We may just be a doomed species. Maybe we all should give up. Quit. Wrigley was right about that. What's the point of trying to communicate when it leads to misunderstanding and violence? Even the smart kids don't get it. And Alex is brilliant!"

He was red hot and raving.

Practically foaming at the mouth.

He was even scarier than when I'd pressed him about the Tackett twins.

Suddenly, Booker was sounding a lot like all the other adults in my life—defensive, exhausted, resigned—and I didn't like it. It made me trust him less. And depressed the hell out of me.

"I'm going to go now, Booker. Okay?"

"Very well. Just go home, then. Quit on me! And never come back. I'm no good for your type—youth."

I was stunned. "Are you defriending me? Like, in real life?"

"In light of recent events, what else is there to do? I'll spare us both any further difficulties. You and me—we're finished," he said, in a way that was mean. Palms up. Shoulders raised. Eyes squinted. I could feel the anxiety and frustration coming off him. I needed to get away, which was a new feeling, because I had always felt calm around Booker before—drawn to him.

I shrugged and then left.

My eyes started to water on the ride home—and it wasn't because of the wind.

When I arrived at my house, my father was in our living room, sitting on the opposite side of the same white couch my mother was occupying.

132

"Why did you skip school?" they said, almost in unison. "Where have you been?"

"You know what? I'm going to tell you the truth," I said, and then I erupted, telling them everything—from Shannon spreading rumors about me being a lesbian, my hatred of soccer, my love of *The Bubblegum Reaper*, kissing Mr. Graves, how practically all the girls on the soccer team were alcoholic sexpots, my love affair with Alex, his defending little kids and ending up in jail, all the way to my not being sure that I actually even wanted to go to college next year. "The truth is I'm not sure about *anything* anymore. I have no idea what I want to do tomorrow let alone next year or any year after that and now you two are splitting up and it's like I'm starting from scratch with absolutely no map and I'm scared, okay! *I'm fucking scared!*"

I started ugly crying, and I couldn't stop.

It felt like so many years' worth of anxiety and worry were trying to escape all at once—maybe like an emotional volcano, only my mom and dad, they didn't run away to save themselves but sprinted right into my lava. They both jumped up off the couch and wrapped their arms around me even though it meant touching each other. We stayed like that for a long time, and it felt good—almost enough to justify everything that had precipitated it, but not quite.

Later, in my room, I looked up the word *obtuse*.

Imperceptive is a synonym.

Maybe I was obtuse.

18

My Fist Rattling the Skull

THERE IS POWER IN KNOWING

By Alex Redmer

I went to the homes of four fathers
Whose boys were terrorizing
A friend of mine
And I said, "Can you make it stop?"
"Make WHAT stop?" they said
"The terrorizing," I said
All four laughed like I had
Told the greatest joke
Next, platitudes were offered
Like cricket-sized Band-Aids

To the bleeding man
Whose hand has been cut off
"Boys will be boys"
"Kids need to learn to fend for themselves"
"Just part of growing up"
"There are two sides to every story"
"Not my boy"
"What did he do to provoke them?"
And when the little terrorizers
Were forced to face me
They proved to be liars gifted well
Beyond their years
Who could light up their parents' faces
With a powerful, blinding pride
The glow of which
Couldn't be beat
And it was then that I
Realized why these pretty boys
Felt invincible, because
I envied the way their fathers
Believed in them, defended them
Even though they were lying
So when I realized I had lost
And would continue to lose
Forever and ever and ever
I took a swing at the fourth
Father—having already endured
The first three, whose bleached teeth

Glistened in mockery
Which needed to be answered
And spit flew from his mouth
When his head jerked back
My fist rattling the skull
Of that pretty man maker of pretty boys
He dropped to his knees
No longer seeing the glow
And his son began to cry
Like pretty boys do
As I asked him how it felt to
See someone you loved hurt
He had no answer
Of course
Because he had never known
Before
But
Now
He
Knows
There is power in knowing
And I'm sure his pretty boy friends
Now
Know
Too

PART TWO

19

Kill the *I*

Alex is being sent to a school for troubled boys in western Pennsylvania. In orange crayon, he writes me a multipage letter and sends it via the United States Postal Service. The words are scrawled much too big and messy and wild and heavy-handed, and say that Alex is technically not allowed to communicate with me (or anyone) now. His iPhone and computer have been confiscated by his father, who is also selling his Jeep. Alex was made to apologize to Mr. Mandrake, who agreed to drop the assault and harassment charges if Alex leaves for reform school immediately and stays there for at least the remainder of the school year. Reform school costs a lot of money, Alex's father keeps saying over and over again. "Roughly the cost of a brand-new Jeep."

What else is there to say? Alex writes toward the end. *Should I ask you to wait for me like I'm a soldier headed to war? I don't know what will happen to me "out west." (Maybe I am like a prospector chasing gold, leaving his lady behind? Ha-ha!) I've been told that I can "earn" the right to communicate with the outside world but will not be able to do that for at least six weeks from my "start date" and maybe even longer if I do not reform, which I am unlikely to do! I'm going to have to sneak this letter into the mail when my dad isn't looking. He thinks you're a bad influence on me. Hilarious! Especially since I know you don't approve of my choices. You AGREE with my dad. But that's adults. Senseless people. I don't regret what I did. Maybe that's the problem. I don't know. I do already regret not being able to see you. I really do love you, Nanette. You are the best thing that has happened to me in quite some time. You are perfect just the way you are. The first flawless woman I've ever met. I'll contact you when I can, but I completely understand if you can't wait around for me. Can you look in on Oliver and maybe take him to see Sandra Tackett again? Solve the mystery of* The Bubblegum Reaper, *if only for the kid. Maybe you two can go to the movies—the good kind that they show at the art houses in Philly. Or take him to finally meet Booker, if you can talk the old man into it. I don't think the pretty boys will be messing around with Oliver anymore. I'm happy to do time if it means putting the pretty boys in their place. And in the meantime (MEAN TIME! Get it?), don't let the bastards get you down!!!!!!!*

There is a short poem added on as a P.S.

ZOO MAN EXHIBIT

By Alex Redmer

Lions, giraffes, zebras
King cobras, gorillas, camels
Elephants, tigers, polar bears
Killer whales, dolphins, eagles
Llamas, cheetahs, orangutans
Giant pandas, springboks, ostriches
Etc. Etc. Etc. Etc. Etc. Etc. Etc.
We cage and display
All the animals in the world
Regardless of what they do
But maybe it's only the best of men
Who refuse to behave
The ones who take a stand
Who get locked away
(Animals unite!)

What am I supposed to do with those mad words?

Alex's act of violence and departure from me—do those make my first boyfriend one of the bastards, too?

I don't know.

But I don't want to date someone who punches other people's dads in the face and then gets sent to reform school.

I do not want to date a "Zoo Man" locked away, even if he does think I'm "flawless."

I thought I knew Alex, and what we had felt so right. For a

while there, I was never surer about anything in my entire life. But Alex wasn't who he seemed to be at first, which ironically is exactly what he claims to be against—posturing, or "pageantry," as Wrigley says.

My parents are up to speed now thanks to my screaming fit and have been very attentive—concerned enough to take me to see a therapist named Dr. June Westerfeld, who is youngish and insists on being called June instead of Dr. Westerfeld. June is skinny with long dirty-blond hair and vivid green eyes, and she wears tight yoga pants that show off her strong, well-shaped legs and tight sweaters that enhance the look of her small, young-looking boobs, and she also wears the perfect amount of makeup, which highlights her stunning cheekbones without drawing too much attention—all of which makes it hard to like this woman at first, especially because she has a well-respected practice in Center City Philadelphia, right around Rittenhouse Square, and seems to have everything figured out, unlike me, Nanette O'Hare, who has absolutely nothing solved. And so our conversations are very awkward at first. June asks endless questions, and I watch clouds pass by through the fourteenth-floor window. I'm not really trying to be a bitch; I just don't have many answers these days.

If words are air, I'm a flat tire.

There is talk about me being an introvert and having a rebel personality that I had previously suppressed.

When asked if in general it's true that I do not like my class-mates, I think, *It's like she's asking if I have ten fingers as she looks at*

my hands or whether I require the regular intake of air through my
nose or mouth as she watches me breathe.

And yet I nod with enthusiasm.

Just to be a bitch, I ask June why the word *therapist* can be changed to *the rapist* simply by adding a space after the *e*. "Do you rape minds?"

Without breaking eye contact, June says she won't waste time on pointless games meant to distract from the work at hand and looks displeased as we end our second session.

June asks about *The Bubblegum Reaper* during my third visit, which lets me know that my parents have been filling in the blanks when I'm asked to sit in the waiting room at the end of my sessions, because I haven't mentioned my favorite novel once during the first few appointments. Apparently, June would like to read *The Bubblegum Reaper*; this surprises but greatly pleases me. As a missionary for true good literature, I can't help it. And because I have Mr. Graves's paperback copy on me, we decide to photocopy all 227 pages right there in June's office, disregarding the legalese printed at the beginning of the book, violating copyright law with authentic rebel fuck-all glee as the machine flashes repetitively and churns out pages full of a much younger Booker's words.

I enjoy our photocopying the novel more than seems reasonable, although I'm not sure why. Mine is almost a religious zeal. Maybe literature is my religion? Can being a missionary for fiction become my vocation? Maybe engaging with true art is a revolutionary act, as Mr. Graves once suggested. Booker may believe that there is no such thing as fiction, but Nanette O'Hare, well, she believes.

For some reason, I start talking about Alex, telling June everything as we work. My parents pay three hundred dollars for the hour-long session even though we don't do anything except make illegal photocopies and discuss my love life. *Can such therapy actually help?* June's willingness to read *The Bubblegum Reaper* makes her seem a bit hipper than I originally thought. I wonder why my parents have not asked to read Booker's novel. My parents are not rebels, I decide, and that is part of the problem, although I want my parents to be stable and remain committed to the very conventional idea of marriage until death do they part. The irony is not lost on me.

During the fourth session, proving that she actually read Booker's masterpiece, June asks which of Booker's characters I most identify with, saying, "Wrigley? The elementary school kids who spun the turtle around with sticks? One of the twins? The faceless masses of classmates? The teachers? The parents? Or maybe could it be—"

"Unproductive Ted," I say with great assuredness. "I'm the turtle."

"Which makes Alex your Wrigley."

"He'd certainly say so. He tried very hard to emulate his favorite fictional hero."

"So why does Unproductive Ted bite Wrigley? If you're the turtle, certainly you can tell me."

I hadn't really thought much about that before.

And I'm not really sure I'm comfortable with how this metaphor is playing out.

At the end of the novel, Unproductive Ted is dizzy and disoriented, yes, but maybe it's because he can't tell the difference between the little boys who terrorize him and Wrigley, who terrorizes the little boys.

Maybe after so many bad experiences with humans, a hand is simply a hand.

"Are you trying to say that Alex is no better than the boys who use violence to get what they want?" I say to June. "I already know that, okay? I'm not a fucking idiot."

I've become quite fond of cursing.

Fuck.

Fuck.

Fuck.

Fuck.

Fuck.

"But how do you feel? You as Unproductive Ted. *Unproductive Nanette*, if you will. Your intelligence is not in question today. But your feelings—those are a bit more nebulous, to me at least."

Nebulous.

I think of myself as some hazy, distant galaxy stretched across the night sky and then say, "Like I've been spun around on the back of my shell for too many years. I feel positively dizzy. As if life is a blur and the merry-go-round keeps spinning faster and faster. Sometimes it's hard for me to hang on to the horse or pole. And I want to bite just about every fucking hand that extends toward me because I can no longer tell which are good and which are bad. Maybe like there isn't good and bad anymore. *Do you even know what I mean?*"

This leads to a discussion about all the many people in my life—most of whom have not taken my feelings into consideration or "have failed to realize that underneath her 'shell,' Nanette is very vulnerable." Which may be confusing to many because my "shell" has historically proved to be very strong. It protected me for eighteen years before it failed. June says, "Eighteen years is a long time. It's your whole life. And maybe everyone just started to take that shell for granted. How could they have known that it wouldn't hold forever? I'm not sure you even knew. *Did you?*"

I didn't know. I laugh at that little epiphany. It feels good to laugh. I like the way June has turned my failure into an accomplishment using nothing more than words. At least she gives me credit for surviving the first eighteen years of my life. Credit lessens my desire to say *fuck* so much.

June suggests "something that may seem a little weird at first." I'm asked to kill the *I* in my mind. At first, I think she's suggesting that there is an eye or eyeball in my brain, but it turns out that June means the first-person *I*.

"We live in our heads, Nanette, which can be very scary places. We forget that we are not just an *I*, but a *she* and a *you*, too. We forget to see ourselves as others see us. For some people, the problem is narcissism—meaning they are selfish, too self-absorbed. But I think that your problem is that you are too self*less*. You care about the needs of others more than you care about your own needs. You are strong for them even when it's a detriment to your own well-being."

"Then why would I have quit the soccer team when I was the

leading scorer and everyone else wanted me to play?" I say, perhaps a bit too proudly. "I absolutely did that for myself."

"Maybe you only quit when you were too exhausted to continue? Maybe you did what everyone else wanted you to do for so long by playing and scoring goals—you were so strong for others—that you finally just reached a breaking point and, well, you broke. And it was then—*and only then*—that you were able to quit. It wasn't really a choice in the end, but like refusing to pay for your friends' lunches only when you have run out of money. The cursing. The middle fingers in the air. Hardly evidence of a rational, measured decision. Much like Alex, who just started punching people. Do you find it odd that he gets himself sent to reform school just as soon as your relationship is blossoming? Just when you are about to end the mystery of *The Bubblegum Reaper*? A little self-sabotaging, maybe?"

It makes sense.

"And Booker, who published a masterpiece—got good reviews even in major papers—and then pulled his book from the shelves just a year later," I say. "Same thing. So why am I pulled toward men who do this?"

"Maybe because you do it, too? Quitting soccer just before you are about to set a record. Deciding not to go to college just when you are about to receive a scholarship. *See a pattern?*"

I don't like the pattern.

And I sort of hate June for seeing it first.

I feel like a big, dumb asshole.

"I want you to do an experiment," June says, and then suggests that I should begin to think of myself in the third person—not as an *I* but as a *she*. "Nanette is very good at making decisions for other people. She clearly sees that Alex shouldn't have done what he did. But when she is deciding for the first-person *I*, Nanette, she is much less sure. So why not live in the third person for a bit and see how that goes? See yourself as someone else. Refer to yourself as Nanette in your inner monologue—the words that run through your brain all day. Kill the *I*. Maybe begin to keep a diary in the third person, too. You are no longer *me* or *I*. You are *she* or *Nanette*."

"I'll give it a try, I guess. Or should I say, *she'll* give it a try?"

"Nanette will give it a try," June says. "Say it."

Why the fuck not? I think, and then say, "Nanette will give it a try. Nanette will now exist in third person. Nanette O'Hare will only speak in third person. Nanette O'Hare will annoy the hell out of everyone by speaking in third person, which, come to think of it, just may give her great pleasure."

June smiles. "Let's see where it takes us."

20

Love Has Not Necessarily Won

Booker does not call Nanette's iPhone, which greatly disappoints her, because she calls him several times, leaving detailed messages and her phone number just in case he has misplaced it.

When she knocks, Booker does not answer.

His exterior doors are locked; she knows because she tried the knobs of all three.

He is inside.

She hears him walk quickly away from the windows.

His hardwood floors squeak.

His lights turn on and off at night.

Oliver calls many times, but Nanette doesn't answer.

She does not return the boy's messages.

She realizes that she is now Oliver's Booker.

Nanette is a hypocrite, as she expects Booker to be there when she wants him to be there, yet she resents young Oliver for wanting the same thing from her.

June says it's okay for Nanette to take care of herself before she begins taking care of other people again. She also suggests that Booker might be doing the same. Everyone needs to take care of him- or herself first. Nanette needs to work on not only taking care of herself but also allowing others to do the same. June suggests that Nanette's parents need to work on this, too, and that maybe the behavior is learned, or passed down.

Her father moves back into their home and resumes sleeping in the same room as her mother, which seems like a good sign if only because it is one less thing that's different. *Stability.* It's certainly ironic how much this rebel loves that word right now. Nanette knows it doesn't mean her mother and father love each other again—love has not necessarily won—but she likes having her father home. He no longer asks her about college or soccer or the stock market, and Nanette is grateful for that. However, Nanette wonders if this means her father is not taking care of himself, but sacrificing his own mental health for his daughter. *Isn't that what good parents do?* Nanette wonders, but she cannot completely convince herself that this is okay. If her father were a true rebel, he'd be long gone.

Nanette asks if the three of them could play a nightly game of Scrabble, and to her great surprise, her parents agree.

They play every night for weeks—spelling words, adding up points, finding ways to reach the colored squares that boost their scores, teaching one another by example the good two-letter words to play, words in the Scrabble dictionary that no one ever uses in real life but come in handy when trying to fit letters onto the board, such as *za*, *jo*, *xi*, *qi*, *ka*, *li*, and so forth.

Nanette wonders if she is the real-life equivalent of such a word.

She comes in handy when her mom and dad want to feel like they are part of a family, but Nanette can't find her use outside their metaphorical Scrabble board, which is sort of falling apart lately anyway and would surely have called it quits if it weren't for her breakdown.

Nanette wonders about the timing.

Since Alex used to attend a different high school, no one at Nanette's school knows anything about what Alex did. And since she already alienated herself from the soccer team and everyone else at her school, she mostly floats through the hallways unnoticed, like a ghost.

If the boys are coughing into their hands and saying "muff diver" whenever she walks by, Nanette no longer hears them.

June says that detachment can be healthy.

That's what she calls the ghostlike feeling: detachment.

With wide eyes and hopeful voices, Nanette's mother and father ask her a lot of questions every night.

What happened in school today? How do you feel? Would you like to discuss anything? What time would you like to play Scrabble? Is there anything you'd like us to help you with? Have you thought about next year at all? Not that we're trying to rush you, because we aren't. We don't necessarily mean college, we just mean the future in general. We'd like to talk about that whenever you are ready. But you have time.

Nanette answers these questions as vaguely as possible, well, except for the Scrabble one—the family always plays at 8:00 PM, which is the best part of her day—but she honestly is glad that her parents are asking questions. Mom and Dad are being gentle again, which is pleasant. They seem genuinely interested and much less manipulative. June has impressed upon them the seriousness of Nanette's situation. She wishes that her family had found June a long time ago.

Nanette also wishes her family began playing Scrabble on a regular basis years ago.

She likes arranging letters on a board, crossing words with her parents, reaching into the velvety letter bag and wondering what she will pull out—each grab is a fresh chance and makes her feel like a spelling wizard reaching into a magic hat.

Scrabble.

It's what the O'Hares now have.

Sometimes Nanette volunteers to put the game away, but when her parents leave the room, she just stares at the crossword puzzle that her family has made and thinks of snowflakes, wondering if any two finished Scrabble boards are ever exactly the same.

Nanette appreciates the visual representation of her family and the time they spent together, the words that they each picked—nouns and verbs and prepositions and adjectives and conjunctions and adverbs and pronouns—that only they, the O'Hares, would have chosen. She takes a long mental time-exposure and then drops the letters back into the pouch, folds the board, returns the box to the closet, and begins to look forward to the next night's round.

21

What Put Her in the Rocket Ship Headed to Wherever She Is Now

After six or so weeks of ghost-floating through school, ten therapy sessions, and approximately forty-two games of Scrabble, Nanette finally feels well enough to visit Oliver. She does this in mid-December. There is a thin layer of crunchy snow on the ground when she knocks on Oliver's bedroom window.

"Alex?" he says as the blind flies up, and then Nanette watches his face fall in disappointment. He opens the window nonetheless, and Nanette climbs through.

"Have you heard from him?" Oliver asks.

Nanette shakes her head and says, "You?"

"Not a word."

"Pretty boys leaving you alone?" Nanette uses the term *pretty boys* only because she doesn't know how else to refer to Oliver's tormentors.

"Yeah. We all had to go to these meetings where we sat in a circle and shared our feelings with the school psychologist, and now the pretty boys are being overly nice to me."

"That's good, right?"

"I don't know. Every day, the pretty boys ask how I'm doing and if anyone is messing around with me—as if anyone else would torture me. It's kind of weird and I think I liked it better when they were just mean to me all the time, as strange as that sounds. Their being nice is like eternally having a boa constrictor around your neck and pretending that it will never choke you to death. Maybe it's like the school psychologist is feeding the boa live rats to keep it full, and so if he ever stops...I really don't know."

Nanette nods and lets Oliver finish.

"The school psychologist, Dr. Fricke, also brings me into his office once a week for a solo visit, and it's always during science class, which I like the best. Why should I have to miss my favorite class just because I am a victim? It's like they win twice."

Nanette nods again.

"Dr. Fricke asks me a lot of questions that seem pointless, like 'Do you miss your father?' and 'Is your mother taking care of you?' and 'Are you ever sad?' I tell him I want to be in science class because I like that period best, but he says he has a strict schedule, which makes me think that he really doesn't care all that much about my feelings despite what he keeps saying."

Nanette is surprised that Oliver is just picking up where they left off without her having to explain where she's been or apologize for blowing him off, but she's grateful, too. She doesn't want to rehash everything. And she wasn't planning on asking for forgiveness, either, especially since she didn't do anything wrong. She instead tells young Oliver all about June and the roundabout-yet-helpful conversations she has in the fourteenth-floor office high in the Philadelphia sky and how Nanette is now living in third person, which she actually enjoys.

"What about school?" Oliver asks. So she explains her concept of ghost floating, and how speaking in third person keeps everyone at bay by freaking them out. And Oliver says, "Yeah, that's me, too. Same strategy. Although I call it Mr. Invisible. And no third person."

Nanette says that she was recently forced to attend a pep rally for the basketball teams—that the whole school shut down and gathered in the gym so that everyone could worship the few students who were best at dribbling balls and throwing them through a hoop. She asks Oliver how that came to be—how did high schools all over the country decide that athletes needed pep rallies to boost their pride and self-esteem? Isn't it enough that people actually pay money to see these kids compete in games? That people cheer from the sidelines? And they get their names in the paper? Why don't they take all the lonely ghost floaters in every high school and have a pep rally for them? Make all the most popular kids in school sit on the hard bleachers and cheer until their asses hurt like hell?

"Here is Nanette O'Hare, who used to play for the girls' soccer team but now does nothing because she is depressed and seeing a therapist. Let's give her a big round of applause! Lend her some of your pep because she really needs it! Band members, please begin to play a corny orchestral version of a popular rap song while Nanette stands at the center of the gym and waves to all the people who are not depressed! Let's really pep her up! *Pep the fuck out of her!*"

Oliver laughs but in a sad, uncomfortable sort of way, and Nanette realizes that she is being self-piteous, if that is even a word.

"So what have you been up to?" Oliver asks. "Have you been hanging out with Booker?"

"He's not returning Nanette's phone calls at the present moment, which has lasted for months. Won't let Nanette into his house, either. He pretends he's not home whenever she goes."

"Why?"

"Because of Alex. His punching that dad really freaked Booker out. Apparently other kids who have read *The Bubblegum Reaper* have reacted violently before. It's somewhat of a trend."

"But you and I haven't reacted violently," Oliver says. "And we've read the book hundreds of times. I bet most people who read the book don't react violently. It's just that we don't ever hear about those people, because they are law-abiding citizens, maybe."

"That's true," Nanette says, and thinks about how Oliver seems wise beyond his years.

"So why is Booker punishing the nonviolent people who *really* get the book?"

"June, Nanette's therapist, says he's self-sabotaging, like Alex did. It means they do things to ensure that they fail so they don't have to deal with the consequences and responsibilities of success. Nanette's starting to think that Booker's kind of fucked in the head, truth be told. Just like Wrigley."

Oliver makes a sad face, and Nanette can't tell if he's disappointed that she's saying "fuck" so much or if he's sad for Booker, who is fucked up in the head. Then Oliver says, "Have you gone back to Sandra Tackett's?"

Nanette has forgotten all about Sandra Tackett, which seems almost impossible given the circumstances, but true nonetheless. In the post-Alex confusion, she doesn't forget that Sandra Tackett exists; she just forgets that they have given her a copy of *The Bubblegum Reaper* and that Sandra has probably finished reading it by now, unless she is a terribly slow turner of pages. Maybe Nanette forgot that there is still a mystery to solve. She suddenly wonders what Sandra thinks of Booker's novel and if the old classmate of Nigel's is able to identify the real-life inspirations for the main characters. Does she know for whom Booker wrote *T.B.R.*? It seems to matter a lot again, all of a sudden, sitting here with Oliver. Like finding a bread crumb in the woods after months of wandering lost and suddenly remembering that bread crumbs can lead one out of the woods to safety, if only in fairy tales. Nanette is beginning to think that her life is a fairy tale—that fairy tales are much more real than we originally suspect when we first read them as children.

"Nanette hasn't even really thought about Sandra Tackett for a while," Nanette says. "But now that you mention her, Nanette should probably drop in on—"

"We could go this afternoon."

"No car."

"I have a bike. You have a bike. And we have legs to pedal!"

There is no end to this kid's optimism, Nanette thinks, and wonders if that is a good or bad fact.

Wild optimism puts a big target on your forehead.

Oliver and Nanette ride their bikes through the snow and ice, which proves to be slowgoing and very cold, but somehow they manage to reach Sandra Tackett's home. Their pants are soaked with slush, and Nanette's socks are wet, too. When she sees herself reflected in the glass of the storm door, her lips are blue.

They ring the doorbell and are shocked when Booker— wearing nothing but an undershirt and boxers—opens Sandra's front door and then immediately slams it in their faces.

"Was that who I think it was?" Oliver says, because he has never officially met Nigel Wrigley Booker, but has seen pictures of the faux-reclusive fiction writer.

"Um, yeah," Nanette says, smiling ear to ear. "It most definitely was. And he apparently wasn't wearing clothes, which is *very* interesting."

"Does his not wearing clothes mean that he is *getting it on* with Sandra Tackett?" Oliver asks.

"Most likely—yes," Nanette says.

After the doorbell is rung five or so times, Sandra appears wearing a silk Japanese-looking bathrobe—*a kimono, maybe?*— and says, "Hello, children, I'm afraid you've caught me at an inconvenient time. Where have you been for so long? I finished the book many weeks ago, but you never came back and, well, your timing today honestly couldn't be worse. I'm sorry, but I simply cannot speak now."

"Booker answered just a second ago, and he was in his underwear," Nanette says. For some reason she remembers a fitting expression from Shakespeare's *Othello*, which she just read in her senior literature class. Her rather boring and average teacher, Mr. Sherman, did not offer an explanation when they read it aloud, and so the joke went over most of her classmates' heads, but Nanette had laughed and jotted it down in her notebook for future use. "Are you two perhaps 'making the beast with two backs'?"

"What's the beast with two backs?" Oliver asks.

Nanette smiles as she watches Sandra Tackett squirm in her kimono.

"Oh my," Sandra says. "Would you children like to return tomorrow afternoon for tea and cookies? Tomorrow would be so much better for me. Yes, it would."

"Sure," Oliver and Nanette say in unison.

"Very well, then. Four o'clock?" Sandra Tackett says.

"We'll be here," says Oliver.

"Tell Booker hi," Nanette says, "and that Nanette O'Hare misses him a lot."

Sandra nods once before she shuts the door.

As Nanette and Oliver pedal through the slush and snow, Oliver says, "I think I just figured out what the beast with two backs is. If I'm right, I really don't want to think about Booker and Sandra making it."

"You're right," Nanette says.

They have to stop pedaling and put both feet on the ground because neither of them can stop laughing.

"I wish Alex could have been there," Oliver says.

"He could have been," Nanette says coldly. "He chose not to be."

Oliver stops laughing and says, "So you're breaking up with him?"

"How can you break up with someone who is no longer in your life? He abandoned us."

They pedal on, and when they climb through Oliver's bedroom window, his mother is there waiting.

"I was worried! You could have left a note, you know," she says to Oliver. To Nanette, she says, "Didn't think we were going to see you again. Have you heard from Alex?"

"No," Nanette says. "Maybe he's not such a saint after all."

"He got those boys to stop picking on Oliver."

Nanette pedals home, plays Scrabble with her parents, ghost-floats through another school day, pedals to Oliver's. They both ride bikes much easier through the newly plowed streets, and then they wait for Nanette's iPhone to read *3:59*, at which point they knock on Sandra's door.

"Hello!" she says, fully dressed and much too enthusiastically. "Come in!"

Nanette and Oliver follow Sandra inside through a living room with a grandfather clock and couches and a glass coffee table and into what looks like a greenhouse but is really a kitchen, the walls of which are made entirely of windows. The red-orange light from the setting sun pours in from all angles. Nanette and

Oliver sit down at the breakfast bar, and Sandra serves them orange tea with cream and lemon-drop cookies. Nanette is reminded of eating cookies with Mr. Graves, which makes her nostalgic and temporarily melancholy.

"I want to thank you for giving me a copy of *The Bubblegum Reaper*," Sandra says. "Just as soon as I finished it, I looked up Nigel in the phone book, and after a very long phone conversation that allowed us both to reminisce, well, we started seeing each other. I can't really explain what happened other than to say we fell head over heels in love!"

"*Really?*" Nanette says.

"It's like I'm a schoolgirl again!"

"So he wrote the book for you?" Oliver says. "You were the twin he was referring to in the novel? Wrigley was in love with Stella and not Lena?"

"Well," Sandra says, "it's not quite that simple. If you're trying to find out the real-life circumstances that led to Nigel's writing *The Bubblegum Reaper*, I'm afraid the whole twins business is merely a red herring. Albeit a weird tribute. Unless Booker is just flattering me, those characters are indeed inspired by my late sister, Louise, and me. He admitted it. Although neither my sister nor I talked to turtles in the woods, and by his own admission, Booker never asked either of us to the prom."

Oliver says, "You didn't confess all your problems to a turtle by the creek? Booker really didn't ask you to go to the prom?"

"No," Sandra says. "Those things never happened."

"How do you know for certain that it wasn't your sister who did those things?"

"Booker told me," Sandra says. "And I knew my sister better than anyone. She was much less likely to fall for a boy like Nigel. Believe me. She went to the prom with the captain of the football team. The quarterback. She was the quintessential popular girl until the day she died. If one of us were going to talk to turtles in the woods, it would have definitely been me. I wish it *were* me and that Nigel had found me back then. I was desperate to have some sort of real, meaningful conversation with a boy when I was in high school."

"So for whom was the book written?" Nanette says. "And why was it dedicated to the archery pit?"

"I don't know," Sandra answers.

"How can you not know?" Oliver says.

"Because I never spoke with Nigel even once when we were in high school. My twin didn't, either. And Booker won't tell me now. He doesn't want to talk about all that, because the person he wrote it for has been gone for decades and he needs to move on. So I'm going to respect his wishes. He says that now that he and I are friends, we can never talk about *The Bubblegum Reaper* ever again. Apparently, he doesn't talk to his friends about the book. And I think friends are more important than literary discussions anyway. *Don't you agree?*"

"How can you just accept not knowing?" Nanette says. "Don't you *want* to know? Especially now that Booker and you are dating? How can you just let a big part of his life remain a mystery?"

"One of the more pleasant things about getting older is that you stop wanting to know everything. When my sister and then my husband died, I think that's when it really sank in—we don't have a lot of time here on this planet. When your time has almost run out, you just try to enjoy whatever you can. To the world, he presents himself as such a grumpy old fool, but really Nigel's a big softie. A true teddy bear. I haven't had this much fun since I was a girl. Who would have ever believed that I'd end up dating the kid who didn't talk to anyone in high school? Think of the most unlikely person in your class now, and then picture dating them almost fifty years later. Uncanny. And it's all because you kids dreamed up some cockamamie theory and brought me a photocopy of *The Bubblegum Reaper*."

"Is Booker ever going to speak with Nanette again?" Nanette asks.

Sandra pours more tea. "May I ask why you're speaking in third person?"

"Her therapist is making her," Oliver explains.

"Actually, Nanette *chooses* to speak in third person. Her therapist merely recommended it."

"Yeah, that," Oliver says.

"So will Booker ever forgive Nanette?" Nanette asks.

"Oh, you let your aunt Sandra handle all that."

Nanette finds Sandra's quick use of the word *aunt* creepy, but she must admit that it thrills her a little bit, thinking about talking with Booker again, and having another family in addition to the one she inherited—almost like a backup family.

As they pedal home, Oliver says, "So we didn't learn jack crap."

"The lemon-drop cookies were good, though," Nanette says.

"Who knew that I liked orange tea with cream?" Oliver says.

"Oliver?"

"Yes?"

"Would you like to be Nanette's friend?"

"Weren't we already friends?"

"Yes. Nanette just wants to make it official."

"Okay, then."

"So Nanette and Oliver are official friends. Starting . . . now!"

"I considered you an official friend the moment you climbed through my window."

The kid's words stun Nanette, mostly because he means them. Is that what the pretty boys were trying to kill in Oliver? His ability to be indiscriminately kind to everyone he meets?

"Don't ever change, Oliver, because you're going to be an amazing boyfriend for someone someday when you grow up. Whoever ends up with you is going to be very lucky and loved and content."

"What?" the kid says.

"Do you think Nanette will ever hear from Alex again?"

"Yes."

"Why?"

"Because he's Alex."

"He is."

"But you don't love him anymore? You no longer want to date him?"

"Nanette doesn't know."

"Okay. I'm glad that we're hanging out again."

"Yeah, Nanette is happy about that, too."

Nanette watches Oliver climb back into his bedroom through the window, and then she pedals home in time for that night's

Scrabble game, which she intentionally loses—setting her parents up again and again for the triple- and double-word scores—in an effort to boost their egos. She imagines that healthy egos are aphrodisiacs and hopes that her parents also begin to make the beast with two backs again on a regular basis—that they might even stay married when Nanette's crisis is over and she eventually moves out of her parents' home. She would like them to grow old together, as platitude-ish as that sounds.

• • •

Nanette cannot sleep.

She can't stop thinking about Booker.

For the first time, as she tosses and turns, she realizes that she is very angry—mad at her favorite author for abandoning her when she didn't do anything wrong.

Mad at him for putting her romance with Alex in motion and then washing his hands clean of Nanette when it blew up in her face.

The next morning, she skips school and goes to Booker's.

Booker opens the door when Nanette knocks, and she's glad to find him fully clothed this time.

He says, "Shouldn't you be in school?"

"School is merely a social construct. Nanette says, fuck it."

"Why are you cursing? And, perhaps more important, why are you speaking in the third person?"

"Nanette's therapist, June, theorizes that first-person Nanette is far too accommodating."

"So you're in therapy now? Was it my book that drove you to a psychologist? Please don't tell me that my book did that. I'm not taking responsibility for you, too."

Nanette thinks about how her reading *The Bubblegum Reaper* actually *was* the catalyst—what put her in the rocket ship headed to wherever she is now, but she knows better than to say that to neurotic Booker, and so, taking a page out of first-person Nanette's playbook, she instead says, "Don't flatter yourself, old man."

Booker looks relieved as he says, "Come in."

Nanette follows him into the living room.

"So," Booker says.

"So," Nanette answers.

"A game of Scrabble perhaps? *To break the ice?*"

Nanette explains that she plays with her parents now. She's sort of maxed out on Scrabble.

"I'm not sure I like Nanette in the third person."

"Get used to it."

"She's much more sassy, apparently."

"And openly sad."

"Oh."

"Are you in love or something? With Sandra Tackett?"

"As unbelievable as it sounds, I believe I very well may be."

"Yeah, Nanette thought she was in love, too."

Booker shifts his weight and says, "I'm having a hard time wrapping my head around the fact that my effort to set you up with Alex led to catastrophe for you and romance for me. I'm so very happy and you are clearly miserable. *What do you make of that?* I feel there must be a moral, but I cannot seem to figure out what it might be."

Nanette shrugs.

"I'm sorry that things with Alex didn't work out," Booker says. "Have you heard from him?"

Nanette says she hasn't and now she's no longer sure she wants to.

Booker says he feels the same way.

"So are Nanette and Booker *quitting* Alex?" Nanette says, just to be a bitch.

Booker frowns and says, "Why do you think people do bad things after they read my novel?"

"Are we allowed to talk about it now?"

"Just this once."

Nanette doesn't know. She says, "Maybe because it upsets the balance. It makes you think and makes you mad. Challenges you. Gives you the illusion of permission for once to be on the outside who you really are on the inside all the time. It's revolutionary, and so, in the hands of rebels, it creates action."

"And some people should never take a stand. Some people shouldn't let what's inside escape into the world. Is that what you're saying?"

Nanette says she doesn't know about that. She's glad that Booker is happy. That he found Sandra and is getting laid.

"Excuse me?" Booker says, but laughs.

"You deserve to get lucky, Booker. Nanette is happy for you."

"I'm sorry I pushed you into therapy."

"Nanette isn't. It's good for Nanette."

"Don't take this the wrong way, but your talking in third person is positively unnerving. It's like a punishment for the rest of the world."

Nanette shrugs.

Unnerving.

Maybe that's a fringe benefit.

Nanette is more comfortable in third person.

And maybe she wants to punish the world.

"Well, Ms. Third-Person O'Hare, I suppose I'll have to get used to it. Doctor's orders."

And just like that, Booker and Nanette are friends again. It is the first time she ever recovered a friend after having a falling-out. Shannon and the rest of the soccer team had lost their first playoff game back in November, and based on the dirty looks they sent Nanette's way the week after, she had become the scapegoat for their failure. She didn't really mind, because she couldn't care less about soccer records, but it also felt as if a door had officially closed, especially when it came to Shannon, who so desperately wanted to please their coach by becoming a girls' soccer champion.

22

Confident and Brash and Defiant

June brings up the expression "a reason, a season, or a lifetime" in their last therapy session before Christmas, and Nanette says, "Booker quotes that in *The Bubblegum Reaper.* 'People enter our lives for a reason, a season, or a lifetime.'"

"I know, but he didn't coin the phrase. It's a cliché," June says. "And sayings become clichés mostly because they are true. People tend to repeat what they feel is real—authentic."

"Will Nanette ever find a lifetime person?"

"Maybe," June says. "We all hope for that."

"Do you have one?"

"Thought I did once," June says. "Ended in divorce a few years ago."

"So love didn't win in the end."

"Love is still out there doing her thing. I'm not dead yet, after all. And neither are you."

"You just used the pronoun *her*. Do you think love is a woman?" Nanette asks.

"What do you think?"

"Never thought about it before."

"I tend to think of love as a woman. The male version—Cupid, for instance—always seems so dumb to me. Shooting arrows like love is a weapon. Although Pat Benatar is a woman and she sang 'Love Is a Battlefield,' so maybe that theory is stupid. Because I love Pat Benatar."

"Who's Pat Benatar?"

"You just managed to make me feel extremely old, Nanette. Look her up on iTunes. You'll like her."

"Okay. But Nanette can't stop talking in third person. People don't like when she does this. She thinks this is why it is so pleasing to her. Maybe another rebel tendency?"

"Ah, you'll eventually stop talking in third person, Nanette. Feel free to do so at any time. You've made great progress. And I think the experiment is officially a success now."

"Why? How can you tell?"

"You curse at me less, for one thing. Your parents say you are pleasant with them. You seem far less anxious. You've made up with Booker. You have a positive relationship with Oliver. And you no longer call me 'the rapist,' which I appreciate more than I should, considering that I'm supposed to be neutral and objective with my patients."

"What will Nanette do next year? What will she do after high school?"

"Whatever she *wants* to do."

"What if she has no idea what she wants?"

"Well, then she's lucky, because she is young. There I go making references to Pat Benatar songs again. 'Love Is a Battlefield.' Anyway, hardly anybody knows what he or she wants when they are young. You're just being honest about it, maybe."

Nanette says she wonders if she's over Alex because she doesn't think about him much anymore.

"And yet you just brought him up when we were talking about your future. That seems significant to me."

"How so?"

"You tell me."

But Nanette cannot. She realizes that she made some sort of unconscious connection between Alex and the subject of the future, but he hasn't been in contact even once since he was sent away to reform school, which is perhaps even more unforgivable than the violence he unleashed. She had written a letter but never sent it because she had no address and didn't know who would read her words if she just sent them addressed generically to the reform school.

June says, "It's okay to love people who aren't perfect. People who still have work to do on themselves."

Nanette nods, but she's not sure she agrees as she watches the snow fall lightly outside the therapy room window.

"Wrigley at the end of the book, when he's just floating on the water's surface—when he says he understands Unproductive Ted and vows to quit once and for all. *Do you ever feel like that?*" Nanette asks.

"Of course," June says.

"What keeps you going?"

"My work—helping people. I've always wanted to go to Japan, too, which I haven't done just yet but will. Also, ice cream."

"Ice cream?"

"I really love ice cream. Especially coffee ice cream with chocolate jimmies."

Nanette doesn't know what she wants or loves, so she remains quiet.

June says, "I didn't know I wanted to go to Japan when I was your age. I didn't know I wanted to be a therapist, either. I thought I was going to be a surgeon, mostly because my father was a surgeon. You pick up goals and hopes along the way. Don't worry, there are more in your future. You'll see. And you will change. Change can be good. Caterpillar to butterfly."

Nanette wonders why her parents have to pay three hundred dollars an hour for her to hear such reassuring positive words, even if they are clichés.

Why doesn't anyone at her school say things like this?

She fears that June is paid to lie—or say what everyone else cannot.

Nonetheless, Nanette likes June.

She really does.

Later that night, June sends Nanette an e-mail with a link to a

YouTube video. It's Pat Benatar performing the song "Invincible" live. In the video, Pat Benatar is confident and brash and defiant and encourages Nanette to take control of her life. Watching Pat Benatar sing and move is empowering, and Nanette can see why June loves this performer. Nanette pictures June singing "Invincible" in the mirror all through her divorce, trying to channel Pat Benatar's swagger.

Nanette watches the video several times and then downloads Pat Benatar's *Greatest Hits*.

She spends the entire night listening to Pat's huge voice.

Pat Benatar has a rebel personality, and Nanette wonders if this means June does, too.

Nanette sings to herself in the mirror a little bit and that helps.

She likes singing "All Fired Up" best.

23

A "Purple Pleasure Bondage Kit"

When Nanette wakes up on Christmas morning, her parents are in her room grinning at her. "What's going on?" she asks as she rubs her eyes.

"Merry Christmas!" they chime as they thrust a small wrapped box at her. She notices that their hands are touching, making a little nest for the matchbox-sized present, like it's a small bird. The wrapping paper is white, and there is a sky-blue ribbon tied in a bow at the top. "Open it!" her parents yell, and she hasn't seen them this happy in a long time, so she pulls the ribbon and peels off the paper and opens the box. Inside is a key. Written in silver on the key is the word *Jeep*.

"What is this?" Nanette says.

Her mother rushes to the window and pulls open the blinds.

"Look," her father says, so Nanette rises from her bed and looks down through the window at a green two-door Jeep. The soft top is down. Nanette asks if it's really for her, and her mom says, "We knew how much you liked riding around in Alex's Jeep, so we got you your own. You'll need a car next year, whatever you decide to do. This will give you a little more independence."

Before she knows what's happening, Nanette and her parents are bundling up in jackets, scarves, mittens, hats, and smiles. Nanette plugs her iPhone into the USB port, plays her new Pat Benatar mix, and then is driving her parents around in the Jeep, which is used and a bit more rugged than the one Alex had, but a lot of fun to drive. Nanette sees her father smiling in the rearview mirror, the ends of his scarf flapping in the wind. She looks over at her mother, who is also grinning ear to ear. Without really thinking about it, Nanette takes her parents to the field where she saw the hunter's moon with Alex. She cues up "Invincible" and goes for it. The field's covered by a few inches of snow, but that's no problem for the Jeep, and so she blasts through the powder with four-wheel drive and feels a wonderful sense of power every time she pushes down on the gas pedal. Her parents apparently know Pat Benatar's "Invincible"; they sing and laugh like teen-agers themselves as Nanette circles around the field, fishtailing and spinning tires, occasionally sending dirt and grass flying up behind them.

A police car arrives with sirens and lights going, so Nanette turns down Pat Benatar, drives over to the road, and the O'Hares all get out of the Jeep. Nanette hopes that it might be Officer Damon, but instead it's just a regular old mustache cop with a flabby belly.

"Christmas present," Nanette's father explains, pats the hood of the Jeep, and then shrugs.

"Neighbors called," the officer says, and points to the houses nearby. "Maybe take it somewhere else?"

"Of course, Officer," Nanette's mother says. "No problem."

"Happy Christmas," the cop says, and then tips his hat.

When the cop pulls away, Nanette's father says, "Just wait a second."

Once the cop car is out of sight, her dad says, "One more lap around the field before we go. *Whaddaya say?*"

"Seriously?" Nanette says.

"Live a little," her mom says. "And put on 'All Fired Up' again." So Nanette hits the gas and they make tracks through the snow, laughing and singing and feeling free, before making their exit.

"So?" her parents say when Nanette pulls into the driveway.

"She loves it!" Nanette says.

"You don't need a boy to have fun in a Jeep," her father says.

"Not that there's anything wrong with having a boyfriend," her mom quickly adds.

Inside, they eat breakfast and exchange more gifts. For her parents, Nanette bought items from the local novelty sex store: naughty dice, massage oils, handcuffs wrapped in pink fuzzy material. She thought it would be funny, but she also thought maybe it would help them find a spark again. As her mom and dad open up a "purple pleasure bondage kit," Nanette begins to regret her choice of presents, especially since the awkward in the room is now palpable.

"How did you know that we were sleeping together again?" Nanette's mom asks. "Can you hear us through the walls?"

Nanette's father must see the horrified look on Nanette's face because he says, "She's kidding."

"The hell I am," Nanette's mom says as she attaches her wrist to Nanette's dad's with the pink fuzzy handcuffs, which simultaneously sickens and amuses Nanette to no end, especially when her dad squeezes her mom's thigh.

"So," Nanette says. "Does this mean you guys are sticking together?"

Nanette's father puts his arm around her mom and says, "Your scare—or whatever you want to call it—you . . . being in need . . . it really brought us closer together. Gave us a common goal. Made us remember that we have something pretty great going on here. Our love made you, after all."

Nanette has a moment of clarity—she realizes that she is indeed the product of her parents' love and that is why she was so worried about that specific love failing.

"I'm over the open-mouth chewing, too," Mom adds.

"I've been trying really hard to chew with my mouth closed," Dad says. *"Have you not noticed?"*

There is a knock at the door.

All three of them look at one another.

"Anyone expecting someone?" her dad says.

"No," Nanette answers. "But Nanette will get it."

When she opens the door, a tall, thin boy with a shaved head and dressed in a jacket and a tie appears and says, "I like your Jeep. But you might want to put the top up. It's snowing a little out here."

It takes her a moment to mentally add the weight and hair so that she can recognize him, but then she says, "Alex?"

"It's the new slimmed-down, hairless, preppy, reformed version of me. The bastards make me run seven miles a day—and before six AM. It's insane. And speaking of crazy, I only have fifteen minutes. My dad is watching me from the street." Alex turns around and waves to his dad, who waves back from a black sedan. Alex is hugging a brown paper grocery bag to his chest. His fingers are clenched so tight they're glowing white in the cold December air. "They gave me a choice once I earned it. Either I was allowed to make a ten-minute phone call once every ten days, or I was allowed to bank the time and leave for twenty-four hours on Christmas. I chose Christmas because it meant that I might get to see you for even a little bit. But my dad says it can only be fifteen minutes—no more—and he has to chaperone. He still thinks you're a bad influence on me. I had to tell him I was officially breaking up with you today. I'm not. *Duh.* But I agreed to his terms just to get this chance, so the clock is ticking now."

"Nanette?" her parents call from the other room. "Who is it?"

She is too shocked to speak.

"It's weird," Alex says. "My just showing up after so much silence. And today of all days. I know."

Her parents are now standing behind her.

"Hi, Mr. and Mrs. O'Hare. Alex Redmer here. Merry Christmas!"

"Are you okay, Nanette?" her father asks.

She nods.

"We'll be right in the other room," her mom says, and then her parents leave them standing in the doorway.

"I write you poems every day," Alex says, and then tries to hand Nanette the bag. "These explain everything. Will let you know exactly what I've been through these last few months. I still love you, Nanette. We can be together in the future. We just have to make it through this last bit of our childhoods."

She doesn't take the bag. She doesn't know what to say.

"You're mad at me," Alex says. "I understand. It must have been quite a shock for you. I just saw Oliver earlier. He says you two have been hanging out. He says you're best friends now. Made me a little jealous. Told him not to move in on my woman while I'm locked up."

"You can't do this," Nanette says. "Just pop in and out of Nanette's life. Go all vigilante and then leave Oliver and Nanette behind to pick up the fragments of their lives and then expect them to be okay with your coming back whenever you want."

"I heard about the third-person thing. I think it's kind of sexy."

"Not sexy. *Important.* Part of her therapy."

"Oliver says the pretty boys have completely—"

"But what about *Nanette*? And Oliver has no friends. He'd be all alone if it weren't for Nanette visiting him every day. And *Nanette* is all alone since you got yourself in trouble. You were her rebel partner, helping her through her transition, but then you just vanished and now you're gone! Not fair!"

"The poetry explains everything," he says, and then offers her the bag once more. "Just read them. It's pretty much my manifesto. If you disagree with what I've written, well, then I'll just have to accept that. That's what rebels do. But I think you'll get it. Booker put us together because he knew—the part of him who was once Wrigley saw the parts of us who still are. I have to survive reform school for another six months, but then after that we could do amazing things together. If you can only wait for me. We have the rest of our lives! We can do whatever we want! We'll be entirely free!"

"Theoretically speaking—what will Alex and Nanette *specifically* do?"

"Change the world!"

"How? Nanette and Alex are just teenagers living in average suburban towns. They have no power or influence."

"Everyone who ever did anything revolutionary was just an eighteen-year-old kid once. George Washington, Malcolm X, Che Guevara, Nelson Mandela, Nigel Wrigley Booker. Social status is just a social construct, the primary function of which is to keep regular people oppressed and rebels in line. Read the poems and letters. You'll understand."

"And then? What should Nanette do after reading?"

"Wait for me. I'll be in touch. Trust me."

Alex's father beeps the horn, and Nanette thinks there's no way fifteen minutes could have possibly passed, although time always seems to speed up whenever Alex is around.

"I'm going to kiss you now," he says, and then does exactly that before she can protest.

When his lips land on hers, electricity once again shoots through her entire body, short-circuiting every rational thought in her head, and before she knows what she's doing, she's kissing him back—rebelling against her own better judgment.

"I love you, Nanette O'Hare," Alex says. "Someday you will love me, too—enough to say it back. Read the poems and letters."

Alex winks at her and then he's in his father's car, and Nanette is looking at the taillights getting smaller and smaller down the road, wondering what the hell just happened.

When she returns to the living room, her dad says, "Should we be worried about your purchasing sex toys now that Alex is back in your life?"

Suddenly that joke isn't funny anymore. "Alex isn't in Nanette's life. He's going back to reform school tonight. Won't see him again for six more months, if ever."

"That's an eternity in teenage years, correct?" Dad says.

"What's in the bag?" Mom asks.

"Nothing," Nanette says, and then retreats to her bedroom so that she can read Alex's words, which she does without stopping until Christmas is officially over.

When her parents knock on the door and ask if she is okay, she requests to be left alone, and after several knocks and questions, her parents finally grant that request.

She does not sleep.

She rereads everything several times.

There are no straight-up letters, just poems that are sometimes dazzling or interesting but always cryptic.

Here are the central themes and repeated images found in Alex's poetry: cages, keys, turtles, parents, youth, Jeeps, rebellion,

Independence Hall in Philadelphia, the Liberty Bell, and "the pretty boys" who populate his reform school, which seems ironic, since all of them are there because they rebelled. You'd think that he would like everyone else who is "imprisoned" along with him, but it's teachers and counselors who are the heroes of his poems. He refers to them as "freedom fighters" and recounts many of the lessons that they teach him as he progresses through a "self-selected curriculum," which seems to revolve mostly around *The Autobiography of Malcolm X*.

It seems as if Alex is hiding behind metaphors and similes and symbolism, and she wishes he would have just written her simple letters explaining everything instead of giving her poems that stir up emotions in her chest, challenge her to think deeply, but ultimately explain nothing at all. She starts to fear that Alex is a coward and that poetry is sometimes a mask people wear when they do not wish to be seen or reveal what they are actually thinking. The more she reads, the more Nanette believes that Alex might be losing his mind, and yet there is an undeniable elegance woven throughout the words. She thinks of Hamlet and how Ophelia seemed to make her madness appear pretty. Nanette is afraid of Alex, and yet she finds him more attractive than anything else in her life.

There are no poems about Nanette, and while she is no narcissist, as June has officially determined, it is hard to "wait" for a poet to return when he writes about every emotion he has except his professed love. Nanette begins to feel as though he is punishing her, injecting his every thought into her brain with the needle of poetry but never offering the thoughts she'd most like him to have. And yet, he came on Christmas; he gave *her* his poetry, which seems weighty. He said he loved her.

Of the dozens of poems in the brown paper grocery bag, she keeps coming back to one, called "The Expendable Spider-Man Alex." She experiences a vague premonition when she reads it, although she's not exactly sure if the poem is based on real events. "There is no such thing as fiction," Booker and Alex have often said. And so she wonders whether she should show the poem to Alex's father or send it to the people who run Alex's reform school. Is the poem a cry for help? Or is Alex trusting her with his most intimate secrets and therefore she has a responsibility to keep his confidence? There are almost a hundred poems in the bag, and this was only one of them. Alex surely didn't expect her to read all the poems in one night.

Nanette lies awake in her bed thinking and then rereading and then thinking some more.

When she finally drifts off to sleep, Nanette dreams that she is falling and wakes up sweaty and terrified.

The novelty gifts she gave to her parents as a joke—the fuzzy pink handcuffs and the purple pleasure bondage kit. She starts to understand why people want to restrain their loved ones and why love is so often linked with pain, as if joy and suffering were two sides of the same coin.

Somehow she knows something bad is going to happen to Alex, and yet she worries that this thought makes her just as unbalanced as he seems in his poetry.

After all—it's only a poem written by a teenage boy.

What power could there be in that?

24

There Is Always an Exit Window

THE EXPENDABLE SPIDER-MAN

ALEX

By Alex Redmer

The windows of my cell are unlocked
Because I am on the seventh floor
And they don't know I'm Spider-Man
They think I'm just a regular kid
Who cannot climb walls
They believe that gravity can kill me
And that a dead me is the same as
A locked-up me—problem solved

But the bricks of this building are
Old as the mortar, which has crumbled in
Between here and there making cracks
Deep enough for fingertips
Strong enough to cling, and dress shoe
Soles that stick out just a few centimeters
From the black leather upper
Find their way like hands into gloves
And so I climb in the middle of the night
When everyone else is resting
Up for running and push-ups
First thing in the morning
Before the sun rises over
The eastern horizon
And with arms and legs spread wide
Muscles quivering like
Strummed guitar strings
As a crab scuttles over sand
I rise up the side of the brick face
It's slow going because I
Must rest from time to time
On the pretty boys' windowsills
As the moonlight illuminates
Their sweet sleeping cheeks
I pity them for they know not
What it means to ascend
They lie in beds dutifully

Like pretty boys do
And observing their compliance gives
Me the strength I need to push on
With amazing finger strength and
The awful horrible need
I rise, never looking down
Or caring if I fall—because
It would end suddenly, everything
As I was climbing free for me
And not lying in bed for them
But when I reach the slate roof
And pull myself onto
The toothlike shingles, and then
With my heels in the copper gutters
My head in the stars
I howl out my freedom
Like a bullet exploding
From a gun barrel
And I know
That they will never
Keep me down
Because there is always
An exit window
That leads somewhere
No one else will go
And the gambling bastards
Well, they always leave it unlocked
Yes, they do

25

The Environment's Health Is the Last Thing on Her Mind

Nanette shares Alex's poetry with June, and they discuss "The Expendable Spider-Man Alex" at great length. June understands Nanette's concerns about the word *expendable* in the title and the risky behavior described in the poem, but she says that teenagers often fantasize, and regardless of whether the poem is a metaphor, Alex is in no way taking Nanette's feelings into consideration.

"Did he even ask you one question about yourself when he showed up uninvited and interrupted—and based on what you told me, I'd even say *ruined*—your family's Christmas? You told me about driving the Jeep with your parents, and it sounded like pure bliss, and then Alex inserts his problems into your life, and you end up here feeling anxious and responsible. Can you see how that makes Alex out to be the villain here?"

Nanette can indeed see that, but she also remembers the electric feeling of Alex's lips touching hers and the important way she feels when she alone reads his poetry—words with which he entrusted *her*.

"Do you think this is a healthy relationship, Nanette?" June asks. "Or a fool's romance?"

• • •

"What do you think?" Nanette asks Oliver after she finishes telling him all about her Christmas experience with Alex and what June has suggested. They're sitting on the floor in Oliver's bedroom, surrounded by pictures of flowers. It's early January.

"As much as I love Alex, June certainly makes many good points," Oliver says.

"Are you worried that Alex is actually climbing the outside walls of his reform school?"

"Um, I guess so."

"He could fall."

"Yes, he could."

"You seem unconcerned."

"Ask me how I'm doing," Oliver says, and then smiles.

"How are you doing?"

"Fantastic. Ask me why?"

"Why are you fantastic?"

"A girl named Violet transferred into my school. Her parents are botanists and she knows even more about flowers than I do! We've been eating lunch together every day. It's the first time I have ever eaten lunch with *anyone*! Violet dyes her hair African violet purple and wears little yellow hair things to make her head look like the flower. Isn't that amazing?"

"Are you in love, Oliver?"

"Maybe!"

Arrangements are soon made for Nanette to meet Violet, and when she does, in Oliver's bedroom, the young couple hold hands the whole time in the most adorable way, proving that they are indeed under the spell of love.

"What is your favorite flower, Nanette?" Violet asks.

Nanette never really thought about that before, so she names the first flower that pops into her head.

"What color lily?" Violet asks.

"White?" Nanette says.

"That symbolizes purity."

"How old are you again?"

"We're the same age," Oliver says. *"Isn't that great?"*

"Yes," Nanette says, and then makes an excuse to leave. Oliver doesn't need her anymore. That's certain.

•　　•　　•

When Nanette visits Booker, she finds that Sandra has practically moved in with the now-much-less-reclusive former writer, and they, too, are always holding hands and looking into each other's eyes. It's a nightmare, because Booker won't take anything that Nanette says seriously. When she tells him about the Spider-Man poem, Booker says, "The boy is being dramatic! That's all." Sandra also seems unconcerned.

•   •   •

Nanette's parents begin scheduling date nights for themselves to have some "quality time," which leaves Nanette quite alone with her thoughts. So she takes long drives in her Jeep with the top down and the heat turned up.

She has nowhere to go, no one to visit, and so she drives sort of aimlessly for hours and hours.

June suggests that Nanette needs to engage again with new people—find a new hobby because "driving around is not only boring, but it's also not good for the environment. Especially since you drive a gas-guzzling Jeep." June means it as a joke, but Nanette doesn't laugh. Considering all that is going on—or not going on—the environment's health is the last thing on her mind.

She realizes that her time with Booker and Oliver has somehow come to a close.

Oliver is okay.

Booker is okay.

Nanette is still not okay.

26

He Has Sort of Become a Concept

One year after Nanette kissed her English teacher Mr. Graves in his classroom on Valentine's Day, she's playing a rather unromantic game of Scrabble with her parents when the doorbell rings. Even though Nanette has decided that her relationship with Alex is over, her heart leaps at the thought that he might actually be standing on their front porch steps. She's shocked to find herself running to the door, but when she opens it, Alex is not there.

"Hi—*Nanette?*" a man says.

Nanette nods.

"I'm Alex's father."

He's wearing a gray suit with a shiny red tie knotted tightly under his chin. He's tall but weak-looking, with a long face that somehow reminds Nanette of a stork's.

Maybe Alex has sent more poems or a letter? Nanette thinks, and her heart pounds. But when she notices that Mr. Redmer's eyes are red, she begins to feel as though someone is strangling her.

"I don't know what Alex has told you about me," Mr. Redmer says. "My son, well, he sometimes had a problem holding on to the truth."

Nanette doesn't like Mr. Redmer's use of past tense, and it suddenly feels like she is frozen solid—unable to speak or move.

"Ever since he was a little boy, Alex had this wild imagination— the most radical ideas seemed to burst from his mind. This got him into trouble more than it helped him, I'm afraid. And I'm rambling now. Sorry for that."

Rivers of tears run through the wrinkles of Mr. Redmer's face.

"What happened?" Nanette says.

"Alex is . . . well, he's dead."

"Dead?"

"Slipped and fell off his dorm building wall. Apparently, he tried to climb up to the roof. Didn't make it. Died instantly. No pain. That was two weeks ago. They found this letter on his body. I hesitated, given the circumstances, went back and forth, but ultimately decided to give this to you."

"Because it's Valentine's Day?" Nanette says, thinking that the timing couldn't be crueler.

"I didn't realize it was Valentine's Day. Was it wrong of me to come today?"

She doesn't know how to answer that. She feels as if she must check the facts again, because they don't seem to add up. "So Alex is really dead. You just come here and say that two weeks after he dies?"

"I'm sorry. He's gone. I don't really know what else to say. I've never been good with these sorts of things."

"Was there a funeral?" Nanette whispers.

"No funeral. I'm not religious. Alex was cremated. I put him into the sea. He liked the ocean."

"Why didn't you contact his friends?"

"Alex didn't really have friends. Besides you. And you're why I'm here now."

"Does Oliver know?"

"Who is Oliver?"

"You seriously don't know?"

"Was he the boy my son was claiming to protect? The one whose problems got Alex into so much trouble?" Mr. Redmer says, but not in an accusatory way. He's merely trying to identify Oliver in his mind, although his not knowing for sure speaks volumes.

"Yeah," Nanette says.

"I haven't told anyone but you. Like I said, Alex didn't have a lot of friends. He was sort of a loner, like his old man. Maybe you could tell Oliver? This hasn't exactly been easy for me."

Nanette agrees to tell Oliver and says she is sorry for Mr. Redmer's loss.

"I didn't allow Alex to correspond with you, because I didn't want him to hurt you, but ... well ..."

Mr. Redmer nods and then extends the letter. His hand is

shaking wildly. Nanette takes it, rushes past her parents (who have been eavesdropping in the hallway), and then locks her bedroom door behind her. She opens the envelope and wonders why she is not crying. It all feels too theoretical—surreal, maybe—and not true.

My Dearest Nanette,

I often wonder what you are doing and thinking. It's very strange to have a girlfriend and yet never see or speak with her—no letters, even. It's almost like dating a fictional character whom I dreamed up in my head, like we were written into the pages of a book I read long ago, but somehow that book was taken away from me, and so now I only have the memory of it, with which time plays games, altering everything in strange but subtle ways. But enough of that.

I bet you are wondering why this is the first time I have written you a letter. Well, I'm not allowed to write or receive letters here in this hellhole of a prison unless my father signs off on it, which he has refused to do. (I think he's trying to protect me from you! Hahahaha!) So I couldn't write you one for Christmas. The poems I gave you in that bag when read collectively were like a letter in code and I hope you understood the meaning. My dad doesn't understand poetry so he acquiesced

a little and let me give you the bag because I
said you would help me get them published.
(HAHAHAHA!) I have great plans for our future!

I've made friends with a teacher here—Mr.
Harlow—and he said he would mail this for
me if I aced my Intro to Philosophy exam,
which I did, by writing an essay about you.

I am now writing you by moonlight. Tonight, she's
glowing full and bright as fresh milk—calling to me
like a mother—and I've half a mind to finish this
letter on the roof. Did you read my SPIDER-MAN
poem? (I really do that sometimes. Don't worry.
I'm an ace climber.) The moonbeams are pulling
hard tonight, and I really think I must ascend. This
letter will be much better written if I write while
elevated. The night air will perfume my words
and stuff my sentences with moonbeam magic!

That's all there is. Nanette reads the unfinished letter over and over again, and each time she gets to the end, she's forced to create a little movie in her mind—she's doomed to see Alex trying to scuttle up the brick wall like a human-sized spider until his fingertips give out or his dress shoe tips fail to find a crack and he falls back starfish-like toward Earth and then—*poof*—everything in Alex's mind is instantly erased like a computer that got too close to a magnet.

Return.

To.

Blank.

Nanette tries not to picture the mess that Alex's body must have made, and so in her movie, he shatters into a million tiny pieces like a crystal vase and she pretends to clean him up with a dustpan and broom before she throws all the fragments into the sky, where they will become stars once again. It's childlike poetry that she runs through her mind, but it helps.

June calls it a coping mechanism and insists that Nanette is in no way, shape, or form responsible for Alex's death. Nanette insists that she had a premonition—she knew after reading Alex's "Spider-Man" poem that he was going to die this way.

"That's not a premonition. That's identifying dangerous behavior—like saying someone who drives drunk every night is likely to get into a fatal car crash. Or someone who wrestles alligators for a living might eventually be killed by one. It wasn't the climb that was most dangerous, but Alex's entire way of looking at life. If it wasn't punching the fathers of middle school kids or climbing brick walls without safety precautions, it would have been something else."

Nanette says she should have told someone about the climbing.

"You told me," June says.

"But you didn't do anything to save Alex."

"Alex wasn't my responsibility. And he wasn't yours, either. He was going to do what he was going to do regardless of what anyone said or did. They had him locked up in a reform school. He had been given second chances. People were paying attention to him. He wanted it this way. It's unfortunate, but it's true."

Nanette wonders if it can be that easy. Everyone says it wasn't his or her fault, says they are sorry for the loss, and then moves on with life.

The strangest part is that Nanette doesn't really miss Alex, because he has sort of become a concept. He hasn't been in her life for the past few months. She spent only a couple of months with him to begin with. She's probably spent more hours with Wrigley the fictional character than she did with the late Alex Redmer.

High school students die all over the country—hell, all over the world—every day, and the world keeps spinning.

What does it matter? What do any of us matter? Nanette thinks. *What is the point?*

She very much wants to quit—to sit alone on a log or rock Unproductive Ted–style or float forever in a lake like Wrigley.

Nanette reads *The Bubblegum Reaper* over and over again—like it's a religious text that can provide answers and meaning—but she learns nothing new.

Oliver and Booker express shock and sadness when they hear about Alex's fate. According to his mother, Oliver cries for days. Booker refuses to show Nanette the letters that Alex wrote to him, saying, "They simply were not addressed to you, Nanette." She says they must be filled with clues as to why the tragedy happened, but Booker insists that "there are no good answers for such tragedies and you'll drive yourself mad if you try to find what isn't there." Nanette petitions Sandra for support, but she agrees with Booker. "It's all very sad," is the only thing Sandra says with which Nanette can agree. And then suddenly Oliver, Booker, and Sandra seem to be just memories in Nanette's life—characters in a book she no longer wants to read—and so she stops returning their calls, texts, and e-mails. What can they say or do to change what happened and the way Nanette feels about it?

Absolutely nothing.

One day, when Nanette is driving around in her Jeep, Booker calls her cell phone. Nanette sees a lake, and so she pulls up to the water's edge and throws her iPhone in as it is still ringing.

27

How Do You Turn Tragedy into Something Positive?

A month or so after receiving the news of Alex's death, Nanette finds herself at the police station asking to speak with Officer Damon. The woman behind the glass, Cheryl, asks what the matter is, and so Nanette says, "Remember the boy you had locked up here several months ago? Alex Redmer?"

She frowns and says, "We lock people up here all the time, and you expect me to remember someone from—"

"He's dead."

Cheryl's demeanor changes instantly. She leans toward the glass, her lips part, and her face loosens a little. "I'm so sorry to hear that, sweetheart."

Nanette doesn't like being called sweetheart.

"Nanette would like to speak with Officer Damon."

"Who is Nanette?"

She points to herself.

Cheryl makes a strange face and then says, "Officer Damon is on patrol right now."

"Can you call him?"

"Well, I suppose I could, but..."

"Nanette needs to speak with him about the black ribbon on his thumb. Tell him that's what this is about. It's extremely important."

She looks at Nanette for a few seconds before she disappears into the next room.

When she returns, Cheryl says, "He's on his way. You can wait for him in the parking lot if you want."

Nanette waits in the parking lot because she can tell that Cheryl does not want her to wait in the police station.

When Officer Damon arrives in his cruiser, he exits, removes his mirrored sunglasses, and says, "I'm so sorry to hear about Alex. *What happened?*"

Nanette tells him what she knows.

Officer Damon maintains eye contact while she speaks, and then when she finishes the story, he shakes his head and says, "A shame. A real shame. I'm so sorry."

"So what does Nanette do next?"

He looks at her for a beat and says, "What do you mean?"

"Alex went away and then there was not much communication and now he's dead and Nanette doesn't know what to do with that."

"I'm not sure I can help you with—"

"What did *you* do?"

"You mean"—he looks down at the black ribbon—"oh. Well, I cried a lot. I punched holes in the walls of my home. My wife and I went into counseling. Tied a black ribbon around my left thumb. Decided to become a police officer, like I told you before. But none of it was that simple. You can't always put these things into words."

"Doing all that made it okay?"

"Made *what* okay?"

"Your son's death."

"I wouldn't say it made it okay."

"Then what would you say?"

"It helped. I decided to turn the negatives into positives. As many as I could, anyway. Negatives produce more negatives, and I'd had enough of negative. I was drowning in negativity."

"So that's what Nanette should do now that Alex is dead? Turn the negatives into positives?"

"Maybe you should be talking to a counselor, too?"

"Yes, Nanette is already in therapy."

"I hope this won't come off sounding harsh, but I'm not sure what you want from me," he says. "What can I do for you? *Really?*"

"Do you think Nanette should tie something around her thumb?"

He swallows once and then says, "If you have something you want to remember, maybe you should. It's a good way to start a conversation. It draws attention."

"A form of rebellion."

"Yes, I guess it is."

"You won't let the world forget."

Officer Damon nods and says, "The pain lessens with time. You don't believe it at first, but—"

"Nanette is not in all that much pain regarding Alex's death. She is just sort of confused and lost."

Officer Damon rubs the black ribbon. "Well, for us it was helpful to promote understanding. We went to the jail and met with the man who killed our son. Realized how sick he was, and still is. We asked him questions. Faced our demons. We volunteered places. Now I tell our story to parents of elementary school kids and run programs that make sure kids are instructed on what they should do if someone they don't know tries to pick them up. We've attempted to take the tragedy and flip it around."

"Flip it around?"

"Yeah, for lack of a better saying. Flip it around. It's not easy, but it can be done."

"Didn't you just want to quit? Give up?"

"I drank a lot for a while. But over time, we managed to battle. It was an epic battle. That's life, I guess."

"Why don't they tell kids that in school? That life is so hard."

"Everyone hopes it will be easier for kids. Maybe the goal in America is to have an easy life, and so we find it too disgraceful to tell the truth. I meet a lot of people in my line of work, and I can say with utmost certainty—life is pretty hard for almost all of them."

Nanette looks at the cop for a long time and then she says, "Thanks for being nice to Alex."

"I was just doing my job."

"Bullshit. That ice queen, Cheryl, behind the glass in there is just doing her job. You went above and beyond. It means something."

He looks at his shoes and then says, "Can I do anything else for you?"

"Nanette might need some legal advice."

"I'm not a lawyer."

"Alex, he gave Nanette a bunch of poems on Christmas. One was about how he liked to climb out his window up to the roof, and he implied that maybe he didn't want to be around anymore. He called himself 'expendable.' I didn't report the poem and that's how he died. Climbing up to the roof. He fell. So is it Nanette's fault? Maybe she could have reported his dangerous behavior? To the school? His father?"

"You are definitely not responsible for Alex's death. You're just a kid."

Nanette exhales. "So Nanette isn't legally culpable?"

"No. Not at all. Have you talked to your therapist about all this?"

Nanette nods.

"What does he say?"

"*She* says the same thing you just did. I wanted a second opinion. From someone my parents aren't paying."

"I understand."

"Thanks."

"You're welcome."

Nanette doesn't have the emotional energy to say anything else or even look at this kind cop again.

If someone had abducted her son and killed him, she's not sure she could be as friendly and nice as Officer Damon is, which makes her feel shitty about herself, even though she realizes she should just be appreciating his kindness. And that makes her feel even worse.

How do you turn tragedy into something positive?

She doesn't know what to do next.

What should she do?

Nanette turns and walks away.

28

To Side with the Antigones of the World and Never the Creons

Nanette Googles Alex's reform school and finds an e-mail address for the teacher he mentioned in the letter: Mr. Harlow. She e-mails, and they schedule a phone conversation.

NANETTE: Thanks for speaking with Nanette.

MR. HARLOW: I'm sorry for your loss. Alex was...
I liked him. *A lot.* He was an enthusiastic learner.

NANETTE: Alex's father gave Nanette a letter. They found it on Alex's body. It said he had made an arrangement with you. That you would send her a letter if he did well on a philosophy test. He said he wrote an essay about Nanette.

MR. HARLOW: He did write an essay about you, Nanette. But the rest is a fabrication. I never agreed to send you a letter. Alex, well, he seemed to have a problem holding on to reality.

NANETTE: So Alex lied to Nanette?

MR. HARLOW: I'm not sure it's that simple. I'm not sure Alex ever thought that you would receive that letter. I don't think he planned on dying.

NANETTE: He gave Nanette a bag of poetry for Christmas. There was a poem about climbing.

MR. HARLOW: The Spider-Man one.

NANETTE: You read it?

MR. HARLOW: I read all of Alex's poetry. I was his adviser, so he had to submit all his work to me. We have a self-selected curriculum here. Alex was passionate about poetry.

NANETTE: Why didn't you do anything about his climbing?

MR. HARLOW: I actually did. Had the windows in his room bolted shut.

NANETTE: You did? Seriously?

MR. HARLOW: Yes. Alex didn't like that at all.

NANETTE: Then how did he get out?

MR. HARLOW: He barricaded his door and smashed the window with his chair. The monitors on duty heard it and busted into his room. They were yelling up at him when he fell. He probably fell *because* we bolted the window shut. Ironically. If he had simply kept climbing without anyone knowing, maybe he'd still be here. I don't know.

NANETTE: So do you feel guilty?

MR. HARLOW: I'm sad about it, but no. Alex knew he was forcing my hand when he showed me that poem. He knew I'd have his windows bolted shut. I only did my job.

NANETTE: Nanette felt like maybe Alex's death was her fault because she read the poem and did nothing.

MR. HARLOW: It wasn't your fault. Definitely not. Have you read any of Sophocles's plays in school? His tragedies?

NANETTE: No.

MR. HARLOW: Alex and I had just read *Antigone*. He wrote an essay comparing you to Antigone. He really admired your quitting the soccer team. Antigone—as you will see when you read the play—was a woman who wouldn't yield to men. She did what she thought was right. And I admire Antigone a great deal. But the play is largely about pride and what happens when people are stubborn—refuse to bend. It ends in tragedy, as tragedies often do. Alex didn't get that you have to bend every once in a while.

NANETTE: So are you saying that Alex's life was a tragedy?

MR. HARLOW: It ended tragically. He was very
stubborn. Which is why he ended up
here.

NANETTE: Do you think Alex's death could be
Nanette's fault in any way, shape, or form?

MR. HARLOW: Of course not. Alex made choices.
*A man, though wise, should never be
ashamed of learning more, and must
unbend his mind.* That's a quote from
Antigone. Alex and I discussed it at length.
He didn't understand what unbending a
mind means.

NANETTE: You tried to teach him. But he didn't
listen to you.

MR. HARLOW: He was listening in his own way, I
think, but he didn't give himself enough
time to figure it all out.

NANETTE: What do you mean?

MR. HARLOW: He was impulsive. He didn't think
things through. He just did what he
felt he had to right away. I've worked
with thousands of boys over the years.

Being stubborn is a pretty common
characteristic around here.

NANETTE: Thanks for your time.

MR. HARLOW: You were a good friend to Alex.

NANETTE: Will you send Nanette the essay Alex
wrote about *Antigone* and her?

MR. HARLOW: No. Sorry, I can't do that. He didn't
give me his permission. And now he can't.

NANETTE: Did he write something awful in his
essay that you don't want Nanette to see?

MR. HARLOW: No.

NANETTE: Really?

MR. HARLOW: Alex told me about the third-
person thing. Very interesting. Not many
teenagers could pull it off for so long—
commit to it with such sincerity. I admire
that and I may use the technique here
with some of my students. A different
perspective is a very useful tool. Maybe it
will help them.

NANETTE: Okay.

MR. HARLOW: I'm sorry, Nanette. I hope you will
be able to move on in time.

NANETTE: Nanette needs to flip it around.

MR. HARLOW: Flip it around?

NANETTE: Thank you again. Good-bye.

MR. HARLOW: What do you—

Nanette hangs up the phone—then she immediately downloads and reads *Antigone*.

She admires Antigone, who buried her dead brother even when it was made illegal to do so.

The play helps Nanette understand why most people conform—do what they are told. You must sometimes pay a high price for individuality, especially if you are a woman.

Alex paid a high price for individuality.

But you also pay a high price when you order people to do things that they can't do—especially people with a strong sense of self, people with rebel personalities.

Nanette thinks it is ironic that Alex was reading such a play in reform school, where he was supposed to do everything he was told. It makes her wonder about Mr. Harlow. Alex was definitely going to side with the Antigones of the world and never the Creons.

29

The Shaved Hollows of Their Teenage Armpits

"Hey," Nanette hears. She's in her bedroom listening to her "Alex Mix," mostly Lightspeed Champion and Los Campesinos! It's not so much that she misses Alex—it's that she doesn't want to forget him. And she's reading *Oedipus the King* by Sophocles, too, thinking about fate, when she looks up and sees Shannon standing in her bedroom doorframe. "Your parents invited me over. They said you're not doing so well lately?"

Nanette studies Shannon. She's in heavy makeup on a Saturday afternoon. Did she put on makeup for Nanette, or does she always wear so much?

"It's been some time. I've missed you," Shannon says. "What's this music?"

"This song's called 'The Big Guns of Highsmith.' It's by Light-speed Champion."

"Never heard of them. What are you reading?" Shannon asks.

"Sophocles. *Oedipus*."

"What's that?"

"Greek tragedy."

"Why are you reading it?"

"Why not?"

"Um, today is Saturday. Hello, weekend? It's gorgeous outside. Don't you have spring fever?"

"No."

"What the fuck happened to you, Nanette? You went psycho on me at the beginning of soccer season and then you dropped all your friends, and now it seems like you don't hang out with anyone at all. You can't spend your entire life alone, you know. It's not healthy."

Nanette nods.

Shannon's probably right.

Nanette doesn't feel healthy at all.

"Your parents told me about your boyfriend."

"He wasn't Nanette's boyfriend. Nanette and Alex didn't use labels."

"And the third-person thing—that's doing you no favors at school, let me tell you."

"Part of Nanette's therapy."

"I'm sorry that Alex died."

"You didn't even know him."

Shannon nods, and then she gives Nanette this really sincere look—like a glance from elementary school that she's managed to preserve somehow deep inside. "Yeah, but I know *you*. I'm sorry that I blew you off, Nanette. I was pissed—and I had every right to be—but I had no idea that you were going through all this *stuff*. Your parents just told me that—well, you're not even going to college next year? *Really?*"

Nanette stares at Shannon.

Nanette doesn't know what to say.

Shannon says, "We still have the rest of our senior year. You could be a part of that again. There's still time. Listen, your parents and I have talked to administration, and given all that's happened, they're willing to let you go on the senior class trip next month even though you didn't sign up in time. You can room with me. I want you to. *Seriously.*"

"Even though Nanette and you are not soccer champions?" Nanette says.

"We really could have been," Shannon says. "It's a shame we weren't."

Nanette smiles at how silly that seems now, but right then and there, she decides to do an experiment. All the heroes of the Sophocles plays she's read so far seem to bring about tragedy because they will not bend, but insist on taking action and control, so Nanette decides to acquiesce—to be a joiner for a time, to repress her rebel personality and swallow her pride.

"Okay," she says to Shannon. "Nanette will go on the trip."

"You will?" Shannon says in a way that suggests she didn't come here thinking she would succeed in bringing Nanette back into the fold. "Well, then. Do you also want to come to a party tonight, too?"

"Yes," Nanette says quickly, before she changes her mind.

"You're not bullshitting me?"

She shakes her head.

"Okay, cool. You drinking these days?"

"No."

"You want to drive, then? Give me a ride in that Jeep of yours?"

"Sure."

"Pick me up at eight? The party's at Nick Radcliff's."

"Okay."

"You're really cool with this?"

Nanette nods.

"Can we hug it out?"

"Sure."

Nanette stands.

Shannon walks over to her.

They hug.

Nanette feels nothing but Shannon's shoulder bones jutting into her palms, but manages to smile when Shannon looks her in the eye.

"We'll get you back to normal," she says. "See you at eight."

Five minutes later, Nanette's mother visits her bedroom. "Hear you're going out with Shannon tonight."

"Yep."

"And you agreed to go on the senior class trip?"

"Sure."

"That's good. I'm so happy. You need to leave this room eventually, Nanette. It's not healthy to just...stew."

"Can Nanette borrow some makeup for tonight?"

Mom makes wide eyes before saying, "Of course, but maybe you want to drop the third-person thing before you reengage with your classmates?"

"Maybe. Or maybe not."

"What are you up to?"

"As much assimilation as Nanette can possibly stomach."

Nanette showers and does her hair and applies makeup and tries her best to dress like Shannon, wearing her shortest skirt, a tank top that shows off her boobs and black bra straps, and her mother's fancy silver flip-flops. She even squirts perfume on her wrists and behind her ears.

"You look amazing," her mother says.

Nanette's father says, "You okay? You're sure you're up for this?"

"Yep," Nanette says, and then she's off, driving her Jeep across town.

There are two other girls at Shannon's: Maggie Tolliver and Riley Gillan.

They're all drinking margaritas from oversize glasses in the kitchen and acting drunker than they really are, talking about which boys they are "targeting" tonight for hookups, making bets about dick sizes.

Nanette thinks about how Shannon, Maggie, and Riley were

at the center of their middle school sex scandal and how not much has changed since.

"Hey, look who it is!" Riley says when she notices Nanette.

All three girls get up and give Nanette a big, sloppy group hug that smells strongly of tequila and makeup.

To someone who has not been around these girls for their entire lives, it might seem a bit unbelievable that they are literally embracing the same girl who has been the recipient of their hate stares for months now. But Nanette knows how fickle this crew is. They move like a flying V of geese in the sky—all together. So once one of them changes course, the rest must follow.

"We've *missed* you," Maggie says.

"And you look hot!" says Shannon. "Who are you targeting tonight?"

"Whoever's game," Nanette says, trying out her fake personality, hiding behind eyeliner and blush and lipstick.

"Ohhhhh!" the girls say, smiling their approval. "We like this new Nanette!"

"Margarita?" Riley says.

"She's our designated driver," Shannon quickly says, sparing Nanette the peer pressure.

After two more rounds of margaritas, everyone is in Nanette's topless Jeep.

"Isn't it a little cold for the top to be down?" Riley says.

But then fake-drunk Shannon says, "Don't be such a little bitch, Riley. Let's wake up the fucking neighborhood."

Shannon plugs in her iPhone, takes over the radio, and turns it up.

When the first song comes on, Maggie, Riley, and Shannon dance and sing loudly, waving their hands over their heads, showing off the shaved hollows of their teenage armpits.

The music—it sounds like a British guy rapping over acoustic guitar.

"Why aren't you singing? Don't you know this one?" Shannon says, elbowing Nanette.

"No," Nanette yells over the music.

"*What?* They play this on the radio all the time."

Nanette wonders why Shannon needs to use her iPhone to play this music if it's always on the radio. It's an okay enough song, but it sounds exactly like what Shannon and her crew would listen to, because it's mainstream—common. Nothing weird about it at all, and so the new nonweird Nanette nods and pretends to like it, too.

At the party, there are kegs and bottles and boys and more music you can hear on the radio.

Nanette dances to the angry rap they play. During one song, which is played three times in a row, several boys excitedly rap along about fucking each other's bitches while they grind up on Nanette, and so she crosses her wrists above her head, shows off her armpits, gyrates her hips, and smiles just like Shannon, Maggie, and Riley do whenever a new boy rubs his package against their asses. Because she's pretending to be someone else tonight, Nanette also does a sexy sneer and nods whenever these boys put their hands on her stomach and she keeps dancing even though she doesn't like misogynistic rap music at all and finds these boys so painfully similar—like being surrounded by clones.

As the party advances, the three girls she came with pair off with boys, and then Nanette is somehow alone with Ned Frazier in the kitchen. Ned is tall and handsome in a traditional way— sharp jawline, fit body, long feet, which is supposed to mean long dick, according to Riley—and he's popular and dresses exactly like everyone else considered cool at school.

He's also pretty drunk off beer, swaying a bit.

"I've always thought you were hot, Nanette. But you never come out to parties this year. I always wondered why a sexy girl like you would stay home reading books and shit, you know? I mean—*fuck* books," he says, doing the same sort of ironic TV newsman finger-pointing motion he did during the rap song that was played three times.

Why is he doing that? Nanette wonders.

His face is flushed red.

His breath reeks of alcohol, which also seems to be oozing from his skin like sweat. He's now slouching against the counter so that he's at eye level with Nanette and looks like he might fall over at any moment.

"So I feel lucky to be—um…with you here in this kitchen. Like I won the lottery or something. This is a happy, kick-ass night for me because I've always just wanted to…"

He moves closer to Nanette and then reaches out to feel her boob as he tilts his head and begins to tongue-kiss her.

Nanette thinks about a baker kneading bread as Ned Frazier works her left boob with his massive hand. His kiss is too wet, and he bangs his teeth against hers more than once. But she smiles at him, pretending, whenever he says, "Good?" or "You like that?" because of the experiment.

When Ned pulls away, he says, "That was so fucking awesome."

Nanette nods and smiles some more.

"Why aren't you talking?" he says.

"Nanette is talking."

"You're so cute. I love when you call yourself Nanette. It's a massive turn-on. *Goddamn*."

The kissing and groping continue for another lip-chafing half hour before Nanette's finally back in the Jeep with the now ridiculously drunk girls and—against her will—listening to the British pop star rapping over guitar music once more.

They have to pull over when Maggie starts puking.

Luckily the top's still down and Maggie's managed to aim her vomit outside the Jeep, although some does get on the green paint of the passenger-side door.

The girls take turns holding Maggie's hair back as she emits a seemingly endless stream of yellow chunks onto someone's front lawn.

The British guy keeps singing and rapping gleefully through the whole thing.

They finally get vomiting Maggie into Riley's house, where she's staying the night.

Then Shannon and Nanette are alone, driving through the moonlight with the top down and the heat on.

"You were truly cool tonight, Nanette," Shannon says. "Just like old times."

Nanette smiles and nods.

"I hear Ned Frazier is really into you. Is he a good kisser?"

"The best," Nanette lies.

"How big is his dick? Did you get that far?"

"Hell, yeah. It's three and a half feet long. Just shy of four, maybe. Pretty much the length of Nanette's arm. Could stretch it into a jump rope."

Shannon lets out a little squeal and then punches Nanette's shoulder. "See how much better it is?"

"How much better *what* is?"

"Being normal," Shannon says. "Hanging out with us—people your own age, doing age-appropriate things like going to parties! Hooking up with boys. Dancing! If only you would drink and talk in first person!"

"Thanks for saving Nanette from being unique," Nanette says.

Shannon reaches over and holds Nanette's hand. "Of course. Anytime. *Go, Rainbow Dragons, go!*"

When they pull into Shannon's driveway, she wraps her arms around Nanette's neck, says "It's so good to have you back," and then gives Nanette a big kiss on the lips before she stumbles out of the Jeep and disappears into her house.

When Nanette arrives at her own home, her parents are waiting up.

"How did it go?" they ask.

"Great," Nanette lies.

"Really? Did you meet anyone?"

"Nanette kissed Ned Frazier."

"You did?" her mom says.

"You don't seem too happy about it," her dad says.

"Nanette is happy," she says. "So very goddamn happy."

Mom and Dad look at each other.

"It's good you went out with Shannon," her mom says.

"Yeah," her dad says. "You can't stay in your room forever."

"Good night," Nanette says, and then tries to wash Ned Frazier away with half a bottle of mouthwash and a long, hot shower.

30

So Good at Something She Doesn't Enjoy

Daily life. It's easier while conducting the experiment. Much like ghost floating. Nanette tries to swallow her entire self deep down inside her, where no one can see. Harmless as a benign tumor. And she becomes very convincing, smiling all the time, laughing, being who everyone wants her to be, sitting with the girls again in the cafeteria instead of alone on the bench outside.

After a group-talk with June and Nanette's parents, it is decided that Nanette will go to therapy two times a month rather than weekly. Progress. Everyone loves it. Nanette smiles like a good girl and nods enthusiastically. She feels as if she might be picking up on an unconvinced vibe from June, but maybe it's just her imagination. Either way, therapy becomes a biweekly occurrence, which saves her parents six hundred dollars a month.

Ned Frazier hangs out at Nanette's locker, leaves flowers in her Jeep, tongue-kisses her, gropes her chest, sticks his hands down her pants, plays misogynistic music, constantly rapping the dumb lyrics for her, and since all of Ned's guy friends are doing the same things to Nanette's girlfriends, everyone is generally happy about the sameness of Nanette's romance.

She begins training with Shannon, who is scheduled to play college soccer next year on scholarship, and so they run endless miles together and practice connecting on crosses and dribbling and shooting, and it at least feels familiar to sweat again, to get lost in the routines, and to be part of something goal-oriented.

"You could walk on to any team in the country next year, Nanette," Shannon keeps saying. "You could come with me, too."

Nanette wonders if this was the plan all along—if Nanette's parents and Shannon have made a secret pact.

But because Nanette is experimenting with her new personality, she tells Shannon that she's thinking about it.

"Take the Shannon-Nanette machine to the next level!" Shannon says. "We could be college roommates! Maybe even play for Team USA someday! World Cup! USA! USA! USA!"

It's a horrifying thought, but Nanette finds herself on the spring soccer team again, finishing all of Shannon's crosses, heading and shooting the ball into the net with an alarming ease—like she never even quit.

How can Nanette be so good at something she doesn't enjoy?

It seems cruel.

But Shannon and the rest of the team hug her every time she scores, and her father loses his mind on the sidelines—cheering with delirious happiness.

Money is deposited into her portfolio after almost every game.

31

In Love with a Fake Version

The senior class trip takes Nanette to Disney World in Orlando, Florida. There is a plane ride and buses and much group activity—their class infesting waiting rooms and parks and restaurants. Nanette smiles and poses for pictures and flirts with boys and pretends that she is having the time of her life. Ned and she mostly move with their select herd of friends, but they break away in the Magic Kingdom, during which he says, "Let's see how many characters we can get our picture taken with in the next hour. We could make a game of it. What do you think?"

"Okay," Nanette says, because she is being agreeable.

He drags her around by the hand, looking for what Ned calls

"the classics"—Mickey and Goofy and Donald—and they even run at times, searching for the people dressed up in costumes. Whenever they find one, they don't wait in line behind all the little kids. They just ambush the character, photo-bombing whatever shot is in progress. They snap selfies with Ned's phone and run off.

It's sort of a dickhead thing to do, but for the sake of the experiment, Nanette plays along until park security stops them and gives them a lecture about "ruining the magic for little kids."

Ned and Nanette nod respectfully and promise not to photo-bomb any more pictures before they are let go.

They sit down on a bench near the Haunted Mansion, and she realizes both their shirts are soaked with sweat when she catches him glancing down at her pink bra, which is now visible through her white tank top.

"That was cool," he says.

"Yeah."

"I think I'm in love with you, Nanette. Is that crazy to say?"

Nanette looks down at her lap. It suddenly just got harder to pretend. Ned's in love with a fake version of Nanette. It would be funny if it weren't so depressing.

"Want to go into the Haunted Mansion? It's probably air-conditioned," she says.

"Okay," he says, but he sounds confused.

There isn't much of a line, so they are inside within ten or so minutes. They go through the creepy room that expands while an evil voice talks about death and ghouls, and then they are in the little car sitting shoulder-to-shoulder while ghosts dance around them.

Nanette wishes that the ride would last forever so that she will never have to continue the conversation she put off outside.

After seeing the hitchhiking ghost sitting between them in the mirror at the end of the ride, they stroll out into the heat again.

"I meant it," Ned says. "I really do care about you a lot. I think I love you and I know you've had a tough year and are working through some things, but I'm okay with that and I'm willing to rearrange my college plans if it means we can give this thing a go long term. I'm serious."

And Ned *is* serious.

Nanette can tell when she looks in his eyes.

She swallows once and then says, "Let's just have fun here and now, okay?"

"Yeah, I'm all for fun," he says, but the tone is wounded.

She doesn't want to hurt him, even if Alex would have called him a pretty boy.

She doesn't want to hurt anyone.

But what to do without blowing her cover?

"Nanette and Ned have to get to the meeting place," she says. "It's almost time."

They make their way back to the entrance, and when she sees Shannon and company, she sprints toward the safety of the herd.

That night in the hotel room, Nanette tells Shannon about Ned's proposal.

"It's sweet!" Shannon says.

"He was serious, though."

"He's a boy. He has no idea what he's feeling or talking about. Relax. It's just all talk."

Shannon's never known a boy like Alex, Nanette thinks, and then says, "So do you think Nanette should break up with Ned?"

"Why would you do that *now*?"

"She doesn't love him the same way."

"So?"

"She doesn't want to lead him on."

"My god, Nanette, it's high school. Stop being so serious! Do you think I want to *marry* Nick Radcliff? Spend the rest of my life with him? Fuck no! But I'll happily fool around with him for the next two months or so. A girl has sexual desires that need to be attended to, after all. Senior-year summer. It's going to be *hot*!"

"So Nick Radcliff is just a fuck buddy to you?"

"Of course. We both know the deal. We're having some fun now, but when we go to college, we're free again. Ned's a romantic, which is probably why he fell for you."

"What does that mean?"

"You believe in stuff, Nanette. Some boys like that."

"Ned isn't all that deep, Shannon."

She looks at Nanette for a second and says, "Are you?"

Nanette opens her mouth to answer, but no words come.

32

He Smiles Like a Happy Wolf

Ned becomes more insistent about "loving" Nanette and—because of the experiment—she tries to give him what he wants, allowing him to take her further and further sexually.

She closes her eyes and pretends he's Alex when he begins to do what Alex never did to her, and she justifies it in her mind by saying she should have done it with Alex before he died, which makes no sense when she thinks about it too much, so she tries not to.

And then Nanette isn't a virgin anymore.

It hurts more than she thought it would but is over before she knows it. It's the most anticlimactic thing she has ever done, and it has absolutely nothing to do with love or pleasure for her.

Ned says it's the greatest night of his life.

They do it in his bedroom, which smells vaguely of sweat.

His parents are at the movies.

His nine-year-old brother, Seth, is in the basement playing video games.

Ned rolls on a condom, pushes his way in and out of her for a minute or so—panting the whole time—before he flexes all his muscles, becomes stiff as a board, and then collapses and thanks Nanette repeatedly while she struggles to breathe. Having never been in this position before, she doesn't know when it's okay to ask him to get off her.

When he finally rolls off, they discover that she bled all over, so they quickly strip the bed and wash the sheets before his parents see. Nanette has to teach Ned how to use the washing machine and dryer, because his mother has always done his laundry, so he has no idea what to do. He smiles like a happy wolf as he watches her pretreat the bloodstains and pour the detergent and set the machine for sheets.

They play video games with Ned's brother until the sheets are dry, at which point Nanette makes the bed alone and begins to cry in her pretend boyfriend's bedroom.

In her mind, she keeps saying, "I'm sorry. I'm sorry. I'm sorry," but she can't figure out to whom she's offering the apology.

"Are you okay?" Ned says when he finally checks on her. She's just sitting there on his made bed. "Are you crying?"

"No," Nanette says, wiping her eyes.

"Okay," Ned says, like he's afraid. "Do you want to come downstairs with us now?"

Nanette nods and then pulls herself together so that Ned's little brother won't be worried or upset.

Little Seth mostly keeps his eyes on the TV screen, so he doesn't notice how red Nanette's eyes are, and Ned doesn't ask about her crying again.

33

Coach Seems Very Pleased

Somehow Nanette finds herself at State College speaking with the women's soccer coach, lying about all sorts of things—like how Nanette really wants to play college soccer and how she's learned and grown from the experience of missing her senior year and how soccer is now her number one priority and how much she would love to continue playing alongside Shannon.

They even watch a highlight reel of Shannon and Nanette's many combo soccer scores, which Coach Miller had put together and sent along. Nanette feels like she is watching a fictional character score goal after goal as she sits in the glow of the TV screen in the coach's dark office. Her dad can't help but clap and cheer as the balls go into the various nets.

This new college coach seems very pleased, especially since Nanette's parents have agreed to pay her full tuition, which means the coach won't even have to use one of her athletic scholarships to recruit Nanette.

"We're a family here," the woman says from behind a huge desk in her office. "One big unit. We do everything together. You'll never walk alone on this campus. You'll eat, sleep, study, and train with the team. Once you assimilate, you'll become part of something larger than yourself—a team capable of doing so much more than any one of us can do alone. That's our philosophy here. United we stand. Divided we fall. There is no *I*. There is only *us*. How does that sound?"

"Perfect," Nanette says, and even manages to maintain eye contact before her parents and this new coach all trade smiles.

34

You Will Hate Yourself for It

The night before prom, Nanette cannot sleep and around 1:00 AM, she finds herself rereading *The Bubblegum Reaper*. She hasn't read it in months, and she falls prey to Wrigley's spell all over again, which makes her feel guilty about her recent experiment.

Around 3:30 AM, Nanette comes across a line neither she nor Mr. Graves had underlined before, which seems odd, because it immediately sends her searching for a highlighter in her desk.

And then one day you will look for you in the mirror and you'll no longer be able to identify yourself—you'll only see everyone else. You'll know that you did what they wanted you to do. You will have assimilated. And you will hate yourself for it, because it will be too late.

Nanette turns on her bedroom light and looks for herself in the mirror over the dresser.

She sees Nanette, but she also sees all the little bottles and tubes of makeup she has been wearing, and the electric-blue prom dress that her mother and Shannon "helped" her pick out; it's hanging behind her, on the iron canopy bed.

"I'm sorry," she says again. "I'm so sorry."

35

It Feels Like She's Sitting on the TV Remote Control

On the day of the prom, Nanette leaves school early with the other girls whose parents wrote notes so that they could get their hair and nails done in the afternoon. Riley, Shannon, and Maggie insist that Nanette put the top up on her Jeep because they don't want their hair to get messed up, even though it hasn't been styled yet. She does what the group wants even though it's her Jeep and she prefers the wind through her hair.

A small woman scrapes off the dead skin from the bottom of Nanette's feet. She has her fingernails and toenails filed and painted sky blue. Her hair is carefully arranged and hair-sprayed.

Makeup is professionally applied. She is transformed into someone else.

"Are you okay?" Shannon asks as her nails are drying.

"Yeah," Nanette says. "Why?"

"You're so quiet."

"Isn't Nanette always?"

"Yeah, but today I can sort of *feel* your quiet. It's weird."

Nanette smiles at Shannon's use of the word *weird*.

It's the worst thing you can be according to Shannon and company, but it's what Nanette most longs to be—at least the way Shannon means.

Nanette has looked up the word *weird*, which can mean "supernatural" or "fantastic."

It can also be used as a noun to mean "fate or destiny."

But Shannon doesn't know that.

Nanette's parents take pictures of her in the electric-blue dress, and they seem so happy to see her all dolled up like this, ready for prom, doing what eighteen-year-old girls in America are supposed to do.

She pretends to be happy.

She's still doing the experiment.

She smiles with all her might.

The boys have rented a limo, and when they arrive, all the other girls have already been picked up, so Nanette rounds out the number at eight. After a few more pictures in front of her house—the boys goofing around with rented top hats and canes, acting childish in the most innocent of ways, making the parents laugh and trust them—Nanette is seated on Ned's lap in the limo.

He's stroking her leg with one hand; his other is on her belly. Hidden under Nanette's ass and the fabric of her dress is Ned's erection. It feels like she's sitting on the TV remote control.

A flask of vodka is being passed.

Loud music that Nanette doesn't know or like makes it impossible to have a discussion.

It may be the same stupid song they play over and over at parties, because the boys are—*once again*—rapping about fucking other people's bitches, and pointing gun-shaped hands at each other's noses.

And as Nanette looks around the limo, she feels as if she is trapped like a wild animal in a cage for the first time.

Off to her left, she sees a heavily made-up girl reflected in the window. It takes Nanette a second to realize that the girl is Nanette. She gazes into her own pupils and sees the void that's opened up inside her, swallowing everything like some black hole of happiness—and then something deep within Nanette sparks back to life.

She jumps off Ned's lap, bangs her fists on the glass separating them from the driver, and yells, "Stop the limo! Stop the limo! *Stop the fucking limo right fucking now!*" over and over, until the driver finally brakes.

"What's wrong?" they all ask her.

She's no longer acting the part.

There will be a punishment for this.

Their faces are full of hatred.

Their faces say that Nanette isn't supposed to scream like that.

Their faces tell her to be quiet, sip vodka, sit on Ned's boner, and smile like the other girls in the limo.

She doesn't answer but struggles to get out.

The boys pull her back and say that everything is okay.

Too many hands are on her.

"It's not!" Nanette yells. "Let Nanette out!"

"Where do you want to go?" Ned says. The look in his eyes suggests he's somewhere between confused and angry.

"Let her go. Let me talk to her," says Shannon.

Shannon's man finally opens the door, and I jump out of the limo, kick off my pumps, and start to run barefoot down the street.

"Where are you going?" Shannon yells. "What the *hell*, Nanette?"

When the limo begins to follow me, I cut behind houses, jump over fences, rip my prom dress in several places, scuff my pedicure, until I'm sure I've lost my classmates.

Then I'm sprinting barefoot through the streets like a marathoner, except for the restrictive prom dress.

I'm headed toward Booker's.

When I arrive, I'm soaked in sweat and panting hard.

My feet are bleeding.

I look behind me and see blood on the pavement.

I ring the doorbell several times.

Booker answers and says, "Well, look who it is, my prodigal daughter. *Are you wearing a prom dress?*"

"Why did you write *The Bubblegum Reaper*? WHY?"

"Um...why are you yelling at me? Sandra is inside along with Oliver and his new girlfriend, Violet. We're having the most delightful postsupper tea. Would you care to join us?"

A pang of jealousy hits me—Booker has moved on from Alex

and me to Oliver and Violet. But I'm also sort of happy that Oliver has someone besides his mother in his life.

"You can't just play with our heads!"

"Whose heads?"

"Your readers!"

"Wait a second. Is tonight your prom? Is that why you're dressed like—"

"Yes!"

"And you stood up your prom date. *Like Wrigley?*"

I can see the color draining from Booker's face.

"Yeah. Well, *kind of.*"

"I never told you to do that!" Booker roars. "And I didn't tell Alex to climb the outside of a building, either! I just wrote a story! You can't hold me responsible for everything you do after reading my novel!"

"Well, reading your novel changed my life. And now I'm confused and lost and barefoot in a prom dress regardless of whose fault it is!"

"It's not *my* fault!"

"What do I do now—with my life?"

"How would I know that?"

"What did Wrigley do? After he floated in the creek at the end of the book? What happens next? I really need to know. You owe me."

"What do you want me to tell you?"

"The truth!"

Booker sighs, looks at his shoes, and quietly says, "He grew up, Nanette. Worked several jobs he loathed. Failed as a writer.

241

Was unlucky in life and love. Became an old man. Found Sandra at the end. Tried to help a few kids along the way. That's it. Not really worthy of a sequel, if you know what I mean."

"But is Wrigley okay after the book ends? Is he all right *now*?"

"Depends on who you ask."

"Why won't you give me a straight answer?"

"Because there's no such thing. That's what you learn when you grow up. No one knows the answers. *No one.*"

I take a long, hard look at Booker.

He's just a wrinkly old man.

And he's telling the truth; he really doesn't have any answers for me now.

Everything he had went into *The Bubblegum Reaper*, and there was nothing left over.

I might still be hungry, but that doesn't make him an endless literary buffet.

"Good-bye," I say, and then turn my back to him.

"We're playing Scrabble later. You should come in. I think your feet are bleeding. You should really let us attend to your cuts. Nanette? Don't go like this. Please. *Nanette?*"

I keep walking—every step hurts now—and when I arrive home limping, I tell my shocked parents about the experiment that I was conducting and how I tried to be normal, but it just was too hard in the long run.

My mother cleans the cuts on my feet and gets me out of my prom dress and into the bathtub.

I cry it out in a sea of white bubbles as Mom squeezes a sponge over my shoulders, letting warm water run down my back, and then I'm left alone to weep in private.

I weep for Alex.

I weep for me.

I weep for the end of my childhood.

I weep because I no longer believe in heroes like Booker.

But mostly I weep because I am so fucking tired.

When I finish, my parents and I have a long talk, during which I say that I will not be playing soccer anymore and that I seriously have no idea what I want to do when I graduate from high school. "I need time to think," I tell them over and over again until I'm sure they understand that I'm serious.

When my diatribe is over, my parents look at each other.

Silence hangs thick in the air.

Finally, Mom says, "You're actually speaking in first person again?"

I hadn't realized it until now. "I," I say, tasting the word *I* once more. "I guess I am."

"Why today?" Dad asks.

I think about it for a second and then say, "Because it's time to be me."

36

Squinting Out Her Rage

When Shannon returns from a weekend of postprom partying in various vacation homes down the shore, she's sunburned and a bit bloated from binge drinking. She looks like shit, to be honest. I know because she pays me a visit in my bedroom.

She closes the door behind her, crosses her arms, and says, "Why?"

"Why what?" I say from my bed. I'm seated with my back against the wall. I had been reading an inspiring Bukowski poem called "Roll the Dice."

"Why did you freak out like that in the limo?"

"I really don't think you'd understand, Shannon."

"Try me."

"I'm just not like you, okay? I'm just—*not*."

"What? Is it so horrible to be me?"

"No. Not at all. No judgment here. I'm not trying to...It's just that I don't go to proms, and I...Maybe it's like you're a bird and I'm a fish, and I've been out of water for a dangerous amount of time and—"

"You're a teenage girl just like me. We both grew up here. We're both from privileged white families. What the fuck are you talking about?"

I can tell that she doesn't even *want* to understand me, so I just say, "I'm sorry," meaning, *I'm sorry that we aren't going to connect here with this little chat*, but she takes my apology to mean something else.

"You *should* be sorry," Shannon says, pointing at my face. "You completely ruined Ned's prom. What did he do to deserve that humiliation? Why did you agree to go and then leave him like that? If a boy had done that to a girl, it would have been bad. But for *a girl to do it to a boy*—you completely cut his balls off right in front of his best friends on what was supposed to be the best night of his high school experience. He was devastated, Nanette. I mean—he really loved you. And now every time someone asks about his prom—until the day he dies—he will have to lie or tell the super-embarrassing story about how Nanette O'Hare ditched him before they even got there. Do you think maybe you could have broken up with him in a slightly less dramatic way? Or faked it until high school was over, like I'm doing with my boyfriend? Ned drank himself into oblivion all weekend."

"I'm sorry," I say again because I don't know what other words I can offer.

"You were completely selfish and a total bitch. Next year when we go to—"

"I'm not going with you next year."

Shannon glares at me, and her face turns an even brighter shade of pink. *"What?"*

"I'm not going to college in the fall. I need time."

"Time? Time for *what?*"

"To figure out who I am. What I want. Don't you think it's weird that we're told to do something pretty much every second of our teenage lives, and then at the end of it we're just supposed to pick a college and a major and a career without ever really getting a chance to think about it? You're just supposed to go regardless of whether you know why you're going or what you hope to accomplish. Doesn't that seem *strange* to you? Not to mention all the money our parents are supposed to pay for something we're not entirely sure we even want."

"You really don't believe that anyone else thinks about those things? You don't think the rest of us worry about what college will be like or what major we should choose? My god, Nanette, it's all anyone ever talked about this entire fucking year!"

"But do we *really* think about it deeply or do we just ultimately do what we're supposed to do? What our parents want us to do? What society wants us to do? I mean, do you *really* want to play soccer next year? Do you *really* want to be an elementary school teacher? Do you even like kids?"

"Yes! I absolutely do! I love soccer! It's my entire life! I'm really looking forward to working with kids! I am! Why is that so hard to believe?"

"Well, I'm happy for you, then."

"Why don't you want to play soccer? Soccer is fun. It's a game. And it's better than sitting alone in your room feeling sad for yourself."

"I just don't like playing. Simple as that."

"What *do* you like then, Nanette?"

"I like listening to music and reading poetry and novels. I like seeing art house films. I like having philosophical discussions as I look up at a hunter's moon. I like being alone with one other person, rather than being at big parties full of so many people who you never manage to have a real conversation with at all. I like swimming in the ocean. And I like—"

"I like swimming in the ocean. Everyone does. And I always have real conversations at parties. I talk to everyone there. I like movies. Again—pretty much everyone does. Maybe you're just a snob, Nanette. Maybe you think you're better than the rest of us. You're going to end up all alone if you're not careful. I mean, now that Alex is gone, do you even have any other friends besides me?"

Her bringing Alex into this—someone she's never even met—crosses a line.

"I'm sorry, Shannon. I wish you all the best—I really do—but I'd like you to leave now."

"What? Why?"

"I—" But I can't think of the right way to say what I mean without sounding like a complete bitch, and I don't even really feel like I owe Shannon an explanation anymore. Maybe proms and parties and college soccer teams and traditional learning are just fine for people like her and most of the world, but it's not fine for me, and I don't know how to make everyone else understand that without insulting them, which I really don't want to do. "Again, I'm really sorry, but I need you to leave. I don't want to have this conversation with you."

"Are you even fucking serious?" Shannon says, squinting out her rage. "You're throwing me out because I called you on your shit?"

"I'm sorry."

"Fine." Shannon turns her back on me and then strides right out of the room.

I hear my mom ask how it went "up there" and Shannon says, "Your daughter is impossible, Mrs. O'Hare. I'm sorry. I tried. But I'm simply *done.*"

And then Shannon is gone.

Somehow I know that we will never speak again.

And I'm okay with that.

37

I Truly Hope That Girl Will Be Perfect

Although I overhear plenty of people whispering about what I did to Ned, no one speaks to me at school or asks me what happened. Maybe it's more fun to fill in the blanks with gossip, and so it's like I'm invisible again. It's amazing how my entire class instantly unites against me without anyone even wondering if my motives were legit. Even the kids who aren't friends with the Shannon-and-Ned crew seem to be avoiding me.

I do feel bad about ruining Ned's prom, and so I go to his house one night and knock on the door. When his mother answers, she raises her eyebrows and says, "Takes a lot of nerve coming here."

"May I please speak with him?"

"Okay," she says, and then shuts the door in my face.

I wait there anyway because she said "okay," and after what seems like an eternity, the door opens and Ned appears wearing an undershirt and huge green basketball shorts. He doesn't come outside and he doesn't invite me in. He's trying to look tough and pissed off with his arms crossed, but I can tell he wants to cry.

"I just wanted to say I'm sorry that I ruined your prom."

"Why did you freak out in the limo?"

"I—"

"Wait—you're speaking in first person now?"

"I was doing an experiment. With the third-person thing. Trying to be agreeable with everyone for a time. Trying to be like everyone else."

"Everyone speaks in first person."

"The experiment failed. Obviously."

"So let me get this straight—whatever we had, that was just part of some *experiment*? I didn't mean anything more to you?"

"Isn't all teen dating an experiment of sorts?" I say, and then realize how horrible that sounds.

"Ouch." He grits his teeth and looks down at his feet. "Your apology hurts worse than your leaving me solo at the prom. How did you even manage that?"

"Listen, I'm kind of fucked up right now. I don't know what I want. Who I am."

"Whatever. I'm okay."

I can see how much pain he's in, which sort of baffles me. "You really didn't know that I was faking the whole time?"

Ned shakes his head in disbelief. "I feel sorry for you. I've never met a more selfish person. Yeah, I did really care about you—or whoever you were pretending to be during your *experiment*. So congratulations."

"Ned, listen—I'm sorry. You'll find another girl who will love you for who you are. And I truly hope that girl will be perfect for you."

He looks at me one last time, and I can see his eyelashes quiver just before he slams the door shut.

38

World Population Clock

In June's office, I bring her up to speed and then say, "The thing that really has me worried is this: I don't have any friends. Not a single one left. I don't want to see Booker anymore. Oliver has moved on. Mr. Graves is out of the picture. Alex is dead. My entire high school thinks I'm a selfish cunt because I stood up Ned at the prom. And I just read Charles Bukowski's novel *Women*, which sort of ruined him for me. Have you read that book?"

"No."

"It's just so sad and pathetic—and clearly about him. It makes it damn near impossible to admire *the Buk*. Is there *anyone* worth admiring in the world? Or does everyone let you down eventually?"

June taps her chin several times and then says, "How many people were on your varsity soccer team?"

"What? *Why?*"

"Just play along. How many?"

"I don't know. Maybe twenty-five?"

"How many students are enrolled in your high school?"

"About a thousand."

"How many people live in your town?"

"I have no idea."

"Guess."

"Twenty thousand?"

"Do you ever interact with people outside South Jersey? Have you for the last eighteen years?"

"Not really."

"Take out your phone."

I take out my phone.

June says, "Google *world population clock* and then click on the website."

I do that and find a running count of all the people who have died and were born today. I can see that there are many more births than deaths, and so the world's population is growing by the second.

"Why are you showing me this?" I say.

"What does that information tell you?"

"I don't know."

"Think."

"We're fucked?"

"Why?"

"Global warming. At some point there will be more people than resources. We won't be able to sustain—"

"Yes, all true. But let's try to take an optimistic view of things today. How does it relate to your unpopularity?"

"There are more than seven billion people in the world, and so I am completely meaningless?"

June shakes her head. "No. There are seven billion people in the world, and you have only experienced twenty thousand at the most. And those twenty thousand were fairly homogenous. Your experiences with people have been largely dictated by your parents' choices. The neighborhood in which they chose to purchase a house. Where they sent you to school. And maybe those choices weren't the best for you. Maybe you don't fit in where you are now. But you still managed to survive four years of high school and have a few meaningful experiences along the way. There are seven billion other people out there. *Seven billion.* Are you really pessimistic enough to believe that you wouldn't get along with any of them?"

"But how do I move forward? I have no idea!"

"Sometimes you just have to pick a direction and make mistakes. Then you use what you learn from your failure to pick new, better directions so you can make more mistakes and keep learning."

"So do you think I should go to college next year?"

"Do you?"

"I don't know."

"It's a chance to meet new people, if nothing else. Maybe you need to leave the first twenty thousand people behind."

I hadn't really thought about it like that. I knew I didn't want to play soccer anymore. I no longer wanted to hang out with the people in my hometown, but I *am* interested in meeting new people who were also eager to have real, honest conversations.

June says, "You don't have to have it all figured out now or ever. We're all just bumbling through, really. But you'll find something to be passionate about. You just need to leave high school and your town behind."

"But how?"

"Why not pick something and give it a go? You're lucky enough to have parents who can fund your next few years. You should probably take advantage of that in one way or another. It won't be perfect, but it will be different. And different can be very good."

I wonder whether it really can be that easy.

39

A Price to Pay for Pushing Beyond

And then somehow I'm at my high school graduation, waiting in the gym, wondering when this thing will start so it can end.

I feel too warm in my gown and hat, which is pinned to my hair.

Shannon, Riley, and Maggie are in the bleachers ignoring me again.

Ned and his boys won't even make eye contact.

Neither will my old soccer teammates.

As I look around at my classmates, I wonder if Booker went to his high school graduation; I'm pretty sure Wrigley and Eddie Alva didn't.

Everyone looks so happy and excited.

We line up and they play the song and we march in just like we practiced a million times, and I hate it all more than I even thought I would. But when I stand in front of my metal folding chair on the football field and look up into the stadium seats, I locate my parents, and both of them are wiping tears from their eyes. For a fraction of a second, I'm glad to give them this moment, even though it means absolutely nothing to me. Just as soon as they learned about the real Nanette, they adapted and tried to help me the best they could. And it brought them back together, too, which is so strange. Maybe I should have been honest with them earlier. But how was I to know that being honest would make our relationship so much better? Honesty doesn't always produce such good results. And then I think about how I've never really been honest with my peers, either. I never really let them see the true, authentic Nanette O'Hare. Few people besides Alex and Oliver got to hang out with her. And maybe that was my big mistake.

Old men in suits say the same generic things they say every year, the choir sings "Time After Time" by Cyndi Lauper, and then it's time for the speeches delivered by the two students who had the highest grade point averages.

Salutatorian Janelle Priestly is introduced.

They announce that she is going to Princeton, and everyone except me claps as if Janelle Priestly has discovered how to turn dog shit into gold.

She stands and adjusts the microphone, which squeals when she touches it.

I've never before spoken with Janelle Priestly.

We've attended the same high school for four years now, and Janelle Priestly and I haven't exchanged one single syllable.

"It's a great honor to represent this beautiful, promising, and beloved class," she begins, and then waves her hand over all of us like we're a brand-new sports car she's about to give away on some stupid game show.

Janelle Priestly doesn't represent me, I think. *She probably doesn't even know my name.*

In her effort to "represent" me, Janelle Priestly goes on to say words I would never use and proclaim ideas that I do not believe in, and as I look around at my classmates and the school board and the faculty and the band and the parents and even the police officers gathered at the edge of the field...

Just sitting there, enduring the dull, antiquated ritual of a traditional high school graduation, hurts—it feels like there are flames beneath me heating up the metal chair I'm seated on, like my stupid square cardboard hat is full of fire ants, like this whole fucking overprivileged town is slowly grinding away my eyeballs with sandpaper.

But then I realize that I'm free if I want to be—no one has chained me to this folding chair.

So I simply stand and walk out.

Janelle Priestly keeps speaking and my classmates listen and parents fan themselves with programs and everything goes on just fine without me seated among the crowd.

They probably think I have to use the bathroom.

Or maybe they think nothing at all.

The world doesn't really care too much about what you do

sometimes—as long as you let certain types carry on en masse without you.

Looking perplexed and a bit terrified, my parents arrive at my Jeep only a few seconds after I do, and, by way of explanation, I say, "I just couldn't do it."

My dad gives me this terribly sad look that makes me feel shitty, and I sort of hate him for it, even though I realize he's mostly just confused.

"I don't get it, Nanette," Mom spits. "Why leave your own graduation? *Why?* It's a celebration *FOR YOU*. We've been doing everything you want. We've been so tolerant of your needs. Why did you do this to us?"

"I would have stayed for the whole ceremony if that were a possibility, but it just wasn't. I know that sounds like an exaggeration, but it's not. I'm sorry I couldn't give you that."

Mom's mouth is open, but no words are coming out.

When I look at my father, I can see that he doesn't get it, either, and right then and there, I realize that there's a big part of me that my parents will *never* get no matter how many therapy sessions we attend—even if we have a million and one conversations about who I am.

"I wish I could be who you want me to be," I say. "It would make everything so much easier."

When Mom starts crying, Dad puts his arm around her, but no one knows what to say.

The last of Janelle Priestly's words echo out through the green leaves and blue sky and setting sun, and then the crowd breaks out in wild applause.

The O'Hares are outside the circle now, standing in the street, just the three of us.

"Shortest graduation ceremony I've ever attended," Dad says, going for humor, when our silence grows too loud. "And those things can drag on forever."

Mom forces a laugh and then wipes away a tear, but I can tell she's still mad. More precisely, she's embarrassed. It was one thing to have a crazy daughter in private, but many of her professional contacts were in the crowd tonight—the insecure wives and moms with pitiful sex lives and large houses in constant need of updating.

But I can tell that Mom is conflicted, too. June has explained to her what I need, only Mom can't always give it to me—just like I can't always give Mom what she needs from me.

We stand by my Jeep for a few minutes not saying anything as the next speech begins, and it's like we all know that we've reached the end—that things are never going to be the same again. There is something deep within all three of us that doesn't want to let go of whatever we've had for the past eighteen and a half years, even though that's exactly what we have to do.

"See you at home?" Dad finally asks.

I nod.

When they turn their backs, I open my Jeep door, and there's a mysterious book on the driver's seat.

A young, androgynous-looking face stares up at me from under the title: *The Picture of Dorian Gray*.

I look around, my eyes scanning the line of cars on the street and the sidewalks, but I don't see anyone, so I flip through the novel.

No handwritten note inside the flap, but there is one page folded down. On it is a highlighted sentence. It glows neon yellow.

Behind every exquisite thing that existed, there was something tragic.

My mind starts racing.

Who put this book here?

What are they trying to tell me?

I read the entire novel that evening, and if you read it, too, you'll surely see how it relates to what happened my senior year—how Alex and I became obsessed with a piece of art after seeing some part of ourselves in it and how that obsession began to destroy us and maybe even helped to kill Alex.

But what was truly tragic and what exactly was exquisite?

My parents, Mr. Graves, Shannon, Ned, Booker, Oliver—they'd all have different answers to that question. There is a price to pay for pushing beyond everyone else's answers, and what I'm finding out is that I'm more than willing to pay it.

I like to think that Mr. Graves left *Dorian Gray* in my Jeep as a way of officially saying good-bye, but I bet it was Booker.

Either way, I take it for what it's worth—an end of sorts, and a beginning.

40

Velvety as a Good Kiss

The day after graduation, I put my Jeep into drive and head for the shore. The top is down and my hair is trailing behind me. I'm listening to Los Campesinos!'s album *Hold On Now, Youngster...*, blasting my eardrums with singsongy pop punk. When I arrive, I find parking and then walk to the beach. I have no idea whether this area is where Mr. Redmer dumped Alex's ashes, but it doesn't matter, because this is where Alex and I went when we cut school the first day of my senior year—so it's one last time at *our* place.

With my feet in the wet sand, foamy waves licking my ankles, I pull my iPhone from my pocket, plug in my headphones, and listen to Lightspeed Champion's song "Salty Water" in memory of Alex.

Alex was more of an idea than a true friend or a lover. We never got the chance to really know each other or test our compatibility over a significant period of time. I see now that he was sick—that maybe he pushed his needle too far away from the middle of the herd. But being with him for a short time helped push my needle just enough to free me from the life I hated, what everyone expected of me. And even though I have no idea what comes next, I'm grateful that I'm not signed up for a life that would make me miserable. I'm glad I got to be with Alex Redmer for a few months.

When the song finishes, the sun is setting behind me and there are hardly any people left. I strip down to my bikini and wade into the ocean, which is flat as a lake tonight—almost like a bed someone else made, pulling the sheets and comforter tight, everything neat and tucked in.

Perfect.

The water is still cold from winter and spring, and so my skin rebels with goose bumps, but I push on anyway until the ocean rises up to my chin, at which point I lean back and allow my toes to poke out, feel the seawater creep up into my hair. I float that way for a long time, thinking about all that has happened.

"You still identify most with Unproductive Ted," I say to myself, and then stretch out my limbs, lick salt from my lips, and allow the water to fill my ears.

But you're not Unproductive Ted or Wrigley or any of the other Bubblegum Reaper *characters. You are not Booker or Mr. Graves or June or your classmates or your parents or anyone you will meet in your future. You are Nanette O'Hare—and that's okay, because this existence you're making your way through is your story and no one else's.*

I wonder where Alex has gone. I pity him a little because his story has ended—or is he here somehow in spirit? I mean—if his dad was telling the truth about the ashes, Alex is literally in the water with me. And who knows for certain whether our story ends when we die here on this planet? Maybe Alex really is somewhere else. But where? These are dizzying thoughts—and so I try to concentrate on the pink-orange glow of the setting sun.

But just where *did* the rest of Alex go?

His personality?

His laugh?

His wild ideas?

His poetry?

His smile?

His gorgeous mane of hair?

His need for justice?

His concern for the weak?

His humanity?

His tragic stubbornness?

Maybe it all goes on along with me as I make my way through what's left of my time, I think, and then I have another dizzying thought.

I'll probably never know why Booker wrote *The Bubblegum Reaper*, but his writing that novel led to lives being changed and Booker being happy in love now with Sandra Tackett, which he never could have foreseen when he dreamed up Wrigley's world. And so maybe it isn't the motivating factors that matter so much as simply participating—thrusting your best true, authentic self into the universe with wild abandon. Maybe yielding to our true nature propels us forward into the great unknown, toward targets that we haven't even dreamed up yet but exist nonetheless.

I'm waiting for the stars to pop through the black above, waiting for the future to wash over me like so many salty waves—some as turbulent as my thoughts and some as velvety as a good kiss.

What happens to Wrigley when he leaves the water—after the novel ends?

Answering that question really isn't the point, I decide as I leave the ocean tonight.

I've got to find out what happens to Nanette O'Hare.

Lying down, shivering on the last seat of school bus 161, pinned by his teensy doggie gaze, which is completely 100% cute – I'm such a girl, I know – I say, "You won't believe the bull I had to endure today."

My legs are propped up against the window, toes pointing toward the roof so that the poodle skirt I made in Life Skills class settles around my midsection. Yeah, it's the twenty-first century and I wear poodle skirts. I like dogs. I'm a freak. So what? And before anybody reading along gets too jazzed up thinking about my skirt flipped up around my waist, my lovely getaway sticks exposed, allow me to say there's no teenage flesh to be seen here.

I have on two pairs of sweatpants, three pairs of wool socks, two pairs of gloves, a big old hat that covers my freakishly little ears, and three jackets – because I don't own a proper winter coat and it's extremely cold sleeping on Hello Yellow through the dismal January nights.

I can see my breath.

Ice sheets form on the windows.

My teeth chatter.

Sometimes I wake up because my lungs hurt so bad from taking in so much freezing air. It's like gargling chips of dry ice.

My water bottle freezes if I take it out of my inner coat pocket.

Forget about peeing, unless you want to shiver your butt off — literally.

And it's pretty lonely too.

Because I am holding him up above my head, Bobby Big Boy (Triple B) looks down at me, panting with his perfect pink tongue hanging out of his mouth. His breath stinks like the butts he's always trying to sniff whenever he's around any dog women — BBB's an awful flirt even though he is totally monogamous and loyal to Ms. Jenny — but I want to kiss him anyway, because he is a sexy mutt and the most dependable man I know. He'll never leave me — ever — which is why I don't mind the smelly doggie kisses. Plus he's wearing his dapper plaid coat, which I also made in Life Skills class, and his doggie jacket makes him look beautiful. His hair is mussed around the ears like Brad Pitt, or maybe like he needs a bath, but his eyes are loyal and kind.

As I finish my confession, I keep him waiting, suspended above me, his little legs running like he thinks he's on a treadmill or something. There's no rush. We are alone, we have all night, and Bobby Big Boy digs air running above my face.

I've been sleeping with Triple B for somewhere around a year now. I found him in a shoebox half starved — no tags. No lie. He looked like a sock that had been flushed down the toilet — having traveled through all those gross pipes — only to be spit out of some sewer grate into a wet orange Nike box set up sideways like some elementary school kid's diorama. PATHETIC ALMOST DEAD MUTT, the exhibition would have been labeled, had some little tyke taken it into the science fair. Needless to say, I rescued his butt from the curb and nursed him back to health, mostly with scraps of meat I initially stole from Donna's dinner table until she caught me and started buying BBB dog food.

Did I put up Lost-Dog-Found posters?

I'll put it to you this way—if I ever meet the people who let Triple B get so skinny, watch out.

Bobby Big Boy is still air-running like a champ, and will keep at it until I lower him.

Regarding time, the parking-lot streetlights go out around eleven, and then there is no reading or writing—because I can't risk some curious passerby seeing me using a flashlight. That would blow our cover. With no lights—all alone—things can get quite weird, which is why I like to keep Bobby Big Boy around. But it's only nine-something now, so I'll have plenty of time to do my homework, after I'm done confessing to Triple B, who doubles as my at-home priest, of course, because Father Chee is only God's servant and not God, so therefore, not omnipresent. I have priorities, and keeping my soul white with a nightly confession is high up on the list. I'm a pretty good Catholic; I'm still the big V. Momma Mary and me are, like, five-by-five; I'm a holy teenager of God, sucka! And Mom won't be back until after the bar closes, and maybe not even then. She's gone a fishin' for men, as Jesus says.

"Today, I kicked Lex Pinkston in the shin," I tell 3B, his legs still going like mad, "which I know is a sin, especially since God made man in his own image, so He probably does have sympathetic (divine) shins prone to the unmerciful ache of a swift kick to the holy shin bone, and those Roman thugs probably kicked good old JC in the shins a few times before they nailed Our Lord and Savior to a tree, making Him equally sympathetic to the plaintiff's case, but before you go telling God all about my sin of punting teenage-boy shin, Father Big Boy, let me stress that there were extenuating circumstances. Lex made Ricky echo something filthy again—and I warned that plebian, Lex, like fifty times—so I let him have it. I kicked him square in the shin, and he started hopping on one leg—his friends laughing like hyenas, or maybe apes. Scratch that. Primates are cute, and way smarter than Childress Public High School football players, who suck and never win any games, because they are too busy being morons."

I could be wrong but—with his legs still running—Father BBB sorta smiles at my story, like he might even appreciate a good shin-kicking inflicted on an exceptionally evil classmate—which makes Father Thrice B seem almost human for a second. Or maybe I just want him to be human.

So anyway, what happened was…while I was throwing away my trash, Lex told Ricky to tell Ryan Gold that her "boobies are lovely," which Ricky did, of course—not because he is one of God's special children but because he is a guy who can get away with such things because he is special—and Ryan Gold turned bright red before she started to cry, because she's still a prudish virgin pre-woman, like me, and Ricky just started robot laughing—"Hi! Hi! Hi! Hi!"—like he does whenever he is upset and confused, and boy, did it make me mad. Especially since Ricky knows better, and is trying to earn the right to take me to prom. Donna would be devastated if I told her what her only son said today in the cafeteria.

I lower Bobby Big Boy down to my chest. He stops running

and licks my under-chin in an effort to console me. The weight of him on my chest makes me feel less alone – sorta loved – which I realize might be whack, but we get love wherever we can, right? At least that's what Mom says anyway.

"So am I forgiven, Father B3? Off the divine hook? Bark once for yes."

"Rew!" BBB says, just like I taught him. He's a good little doggie. Truly.

AA, 2009

★ ★ ★

When I finish writing the above essay, I rip it up and sigh. It kicked apple bottom, and yet I had to rip it up.

Bobby Big Boy runs south, ducks his little head, and burrows up under my jackets and shirts, snuggling up against my barely bumpy pre-woman chest and keeping me quite warm without scratching up my belly so much, because he is a frickin' gentleman.

Maybe you think I had to rip up the essay because it was sorta a confession, and therefore private, but the truth is that I trust Mr. Doolin, my English teacher, the guy who asked our class to write a slice-of-life story. He's pretty hip and lets us express the truths of our lives in our writing, gaining our trust so that our words can be more authentic, which is cool of him, because I'm sure our writing honestly—the truth—pisses off some teachers and parents, even though all freaky teenagers keep it real when we can.

Maybe you think I ripped up my essay because I didn't want

to narc out my friend Ricky or those moronic football players, but I don't really care about narcing them out, because when you say or do repellent stuff in the lunchroom, that's public knowledge as far as I'm concerned. True? True.

I wouldn't want to turn in an essay that made Ryan Gold look bad, because she is a nice person, but I would have turned this essay in if Ryan was the only thing stopping me, because sometimes—when it comes to writing—you have to sacrifice the feelings of other people to make a statement. Serve the greater good and all, which Mr. Doolin says almost every day.

But the truth is that I don't want anyone to know that I am living out of Hello Yellow—that my mom's last boyfriend, A-hole Oliver, threw us the hell out of his apartment, and that my mom has to save up some dough before we can get four walls of our own. I mean, it's a pretty pathetic story, and I'm not really all that proud to be my mom's daughter right now. Homelessness reflects badly on both of us. True? True.

I'm sure there are people who would let us crash at their houses, because the town of Childress is full of good-hearted dudes and dudettes. Word. But charity is for cripples and old people and Mom is sure to come through one of these days. I still have Bobby Big Boy, and Mom still has her job driving Hello Yellow, all of our clothes and stuff fit in the two storage bins between the wheels, below the bus windows, so it's all good in the hood.

Except that sitting here with my legs up and BBB on my chest, I can't think of anything else to write about—especially since my original essay was so killer.

The quiet of an empty Hello Yellow can drive you a little nuts.

Bobby Big Boy and I just cuddle until the streetlight blinks out and everything goes black.

I can rest my eyes, but I can't really sleep until Mom gets back from fishing, because I worry about her.

She's still pretty.

Bad things happen to pretty women who have daughters like me and can't afford to do jack crap for 'em, which makes said pretty women desperate for a Prince Charming—only Prince Charmings marry hot young chicks my age, or maybe a little older. Mom's almost forty, so she's pretty screwed when it comes to men. Sometimes I like to think about her marrying an old rich dude, who would act all grandfatherly and leave Mom tons of money when he croaked. That would be cool, but it ain't gonna happen. Truth.

Another thing: Mom's taste in men is akin to a crackhead's taste in crack cocaine. Any old hit will do. And it sucks for all nearby loved ones (me) when mi madre is hitting the man-pipe again, because she sorta loses her frickin' mind—to put it bluntly.

All alone on Hello Yellow, I think about Mom for a long time.

She sucks at being a mom. Emphatically.

She's so ridiculously irresponsible and socially dumber than Ricky—who is diagnosed with autism—but I still love her. I'm a sucker for love and having a mom in my life. Call me old-fashioned, maudlin, or mawkish.

When I hear Hello Yellow's front door being keyed into, I freeze and hold my breath.

Should be Mom.

Must be Mom.

What if it's not Mom?

I'm in a creepy parking lot outside of town; it's full of eerily similar school buses parked in perfect lines. Too much symmetry can be daunting. There are train tracks on one side of the parking lot and creepy woods on the other. Bad stuff happens by train tracks and in woods, because some men are inherently evil, and left unchecked, these dudes will do bad hooey — at least according to such cool cats as Herman Melville, who illustrated this exact point through that evil Claggart character from *Billy Budd,* which we just read in my Accelerated American Lit class. The Handsome Sailor. Budd Boy spilling his soup on Claggart in the mess hall — when Billy does that, it's a metaphor for accidental homosexual ejaculation according to Mr. Doolin, who has coitus on the brain 24/7, and sees a sexual metaphor in just about any old sentence. "Handsome is as handsome did it too." Herman Melville. Funny stuff. Truly. But being in a bus alone at night near train tracks and woods ain't so ha-ha, believe me.

Plus there have been a few rape-murders on the outskirts of town lately and the cops haven't caught the bad guy yet, which has lots of people freaked out and for good reason.

Madman nearby — beware!

Finally, I cannot take it and completely blow any chance I have of surviving an encounter with the local psychopath, mostly because I am only seventeen, and a chick, even if I am a junior now. "Mom?" I say.

"Amber? Did I wake you up?"

Whew. It's Mom. "No. Some crazy lumberjack train conductor was just about to abduct me and make me his slave, but you scared him off. Thanks."

"That's not even remotely funny."

"How was fishin' fo' men, any bites?"

"Nope. Nothing."

"A good man is hard to find."

"Damn skippy," my mother says, like a used-up chippie who will never find her Prince Charming, but you can tell—by the tone of her voice—that Mom is faking something, trying to sound hopeful enough to make her daughter feel as though she will not be sleeping on a school bus forever, so I give her a little credit. She's had a harrowing life.

"Always tomorrow," I say through the darkness, as my mom pats my forehead like I am Bobby Big Boy. I like dogs, so I do not take offense.

"Does your puppy need to go out before I hit the hay?"

"Bob probably could squirt a few drops."

"Please don't call him Bob."

"That's his name."

"Your father was—best to forget him, and—"

"Well, Bob here has to take a squirt, and I have school tomorrow, so can we skip the broken-record talk and get doggie duty over with, please? I can't sleep without my pup."

"Come on, little dog," Mom says, clapping her hands. And Bob bursts forth from my pre-woman chest, widening the neck holes of —like—four shirts, and scratching the hell out of my neck. He loves to piss. It's his favorite.

"Use his leash!" I yell, because I don't want 3B to get lost in the dark.

"Okay," Mom says, but I know she doesn't use the leash, because I'm on it—it's under my butt.

My mom lies to me all the time. She sorta has a problem. She is a fabricator of falsehoods. Or maybe she is just drunk again, which is no excuse.

Sometimes when I am losing faith in Mom—which is, like, all the time lately—I like to think about one of the top-seven all-time Amber-and-her-mom moments. These are little videos I have stored in my brain—all documenting the mom I knew before she sorta gave up on life, before Oliver broke Mom's spirit and got her drinking so heavily.

MATTHEW QUICK

is the *New York Times* bestselling author of several novels, including *The Silver Linings Playbook*, *Sorta Like a Rock Star*, *Boy21*, and *Forgive Me, Leonard Peacock*. His work has been translated into more than thirty languages and has received a PEN/Hemingway Award Honorable Mention. He lives with his wife on North Carolina's Outer Banks.